Love Stalks
A Novella

Doré Bak

Block Head Publishing
Vancouver

In gratitude to
J.N.

When you hear the word *Canada*
or *Canadians*, nothing much comes
to mind—unlike hearing the words
Frenchman or *Englishman* or *Chinese*
or *Spaniard*—or *Yankee*. I realize this
is an advantage. The Canadian is still
free, has not yet been ossified by his
word.

> WALKER PERCY,
> *The Thanatos Syndrome*

Author's Note on Transliteration

I anticipate that many of the readers who are familiar with the Chinese language will find my transliteration of Chinese words strange. Some comments to address their possible concerns on this matter are in order.

The current universal standard for transliterating Chinese words in English language publications is known as pinyin, a romanization standard first implemented in the People's Republic of China. It is based on Mandarin which is the predominant dialect in northern China.

In the novella, the protagonist and his family speak a dialect from the county of Toisan (now a city) in southern China. Dialects of this region differ from Mandarin as English differs from French. Even speakers of standard Cantonese from Hong Kong would likely find the Toisan dialect almost unintelligible. The majority of the early Chinese in Canada have roots from the region consisting of the four counties of Toisan, Hoiping, Sunwui and Yinping in Canton (Guangdong) province. They refer to this region as Szeyap (also spelt "Sze Yap" according to the Oxford English Dictionary). Even as recent as the late twentieth century, there is no standard transliteration of words in the Szeyap dialect.

There has been also a cross seeding of some words from other dialects over the years into the Szeyap vernacular. Some Szeyap words are sometimes replaced by pronunciations from standard Cantonese. In fact the spelling "Toisan" itself is from standard Cantonese, not an accurate romanization of the Szeyap dialect. The more accurate pronunciation is "Hoi San." So the county name *Toisan* should be spelt something more like "Hoy San" or "Hoisan." By the 1990s, the time setting of the novella, the Cantonese transliteration of the word *Toisan* has become widely used even among the Szeyap people.

In the twenty-first century, the language professor Deng Jun, a native of Hoiping, and his co-editors have published dictionaries using a standardized romanization of the Toisan and Hoiping dialects. Although I have consulted with Professor Deng's dictionaries, especially his *Kaiping Fangyin Zidian* ("Hoiping Dialect Dictionary"—my translation), on Chinese words used in the novella, I ultimately choose to apply the spelling of Chinese words as though an Anglophone would use without the benefit of a standardized romanization. It is reasonable that the narrator, portrayed as an Anglophone, would use Anglicized transliterations of words of the Szeyap dialect spoken in Canada through the late twentieth century, the time setting of the story.

1

I LIKE TO SIT IN Chinese Canadian cafes, the old greasy spoon kind, and read Kierkegaard. It's not that I'm a philosopher or anything of the kind. Actually, I'm an actuary's assistant. I traffic in numbers with implicit dollar signs in front of them. The reason I read Kierkegaard in some Chinaman's cafe is that I am fascinated with this Danish philosopher's private life. In particular, I am intrigued with his love for Regine Olsen who was betrothed to him but whom he never married. As a result of this broken love, volumes of philosophy came spewing out of him. I have always wondered what it is like to love as he did. To love a woman and yet to give up all hope of marrying her in order to pursue one's destiny, which in Kierkegaard's case was to assault Christendom through his writings, is both tragic and noble.

Why a Chinaman's cafe, you may ask?

Well, I'm not sure how to answer that. Simply put, I just feel at home in those old places. It reminds me of the cafes my father used to own and run. He himself is a true Chinaman. Mind you, I use the word *Chinaman* affectionately, the way some Americans have transformed the once derogatory term *Yankee* into a sign of pride and identity.

It hasn't always been this way with me. I mean sitting alone in cafes, reading Kierkegaard. I used to read other books, mostly books written by scientists, like Einstein's *The World as I See It*, or books on pure mathematics. The language of mathematics is universal, they say. There is no room for misunderstanding in mathematics. A person's accent does not inhibit his listeners' comprehension of mathematical symbols. (I have a speech impediment that is often mistaken for a foreign accent.) Perhaps that is one reason why I took to math when I was a youngster. In those days, it seemed that I could always be understood by a certain community of like-minded individuals. And those who did not understand my equations and tautological statements? Well, they were the plebeians. Although I would never have put it quite that way at the time, that was how I felt.

This afternoon I sit in a little cafe run by a Chinese couple on a side street near a busy corner of Queen Street. It's called the H&M Cafe, initials apparently coined after the first names of the proprietors, Harry and May Lim. By day it is your typical greasy grill. By night, I'm told, it is rented out to an artsy group who turns it into some kind of espresso cafe with live jazz music.

The air outside the cafe is like a steam bath. Inside, a couple of electric fans offer a slight consolation in the heat.

The menu is very similar to the ones I have grown up with on the prairies and in Toronto when my father used to run various cafes at different times, once in Spitting Hills, Alberta and twice in Toronto. I sit on a stool at the counter. The design on the counter top is speckled with tiny grains of metallic squares. The edge of the counter is lined with a metal strip.

Despite the heat, I order a hot meal, liver and bacon. The order comes with a mound of home-made mashed potato, smooth, with a massive gob of butter on the middle of the dome. I blend the butter into the middle of the potato with my knife so that it looks like a yellow lake in a volcano. With the knife, I sweep the smooth, tan gravy onto the edge of the crater and scoop out some potato, trying not to disturb the lake of dissolving butter. Next I spread the mix of mashed potato and gravy onto a stack of liver and bacon skewered on my fork. The taste is near perfection. The bread crumbs are crisply seared onto the liver and crunch lightly in my mouth. I marvel at the pinkish grey juices at the centre of the sliced liver. The cook is an artist.

On the way back to the office, I have this urge to withdraw money from the bank. I never use bank machines. I prefer the personal touch. Taking my time to fill out my withdrawal slip, I look around to see if Tiffany is at wicket number two, her normal station on Fridays. I'm not sure what her last name is because the name tags in this bank have only the first names of the tellers. I don't know why, but I think her surname is Swedish.

There she is in a black sleeveless dress. Her hair is a wild and unkempt golden halo. This is the first time I have seen it unmade. She usually has it bundled up like one of those ladies in Victorian portraits. And she rarely wears black, but I must admit, she looks good in it. Sort of reminds me of those pictures I've seen of beatniks in the late 1950s. A bit of the non-conformist comes out of her, which I like. She's different from the others who are dressed so business-like, square shoulder pads and all. She has an earthy glow about her, no pretentions whatsoever. Her shoulders are nicely rounded on her tall frame. Praise to Thor and to her Viking ancestors for bringing forth into the world such a splendid creature as her!

I shall be bold today and time it so that I'll have Tiffany for my teller. There's only six in the queue in front of me and four tellers are on duty right now. It's been a month since she has been my teller. This time I'm going to strike up a casual conversation and find out what kind of movies she likes. It's best to build small bridges in human relationships. I read that somewhere in a woman's magazine. Maybe after a few more transactions, I'll work up the nerve to ask her to accompany me to the Bergman film festival later this summer.

I wait. My heart thumps in my ears. Stay cool and calm, I tell myself. She finishes with her current customer and her next customer is this little old lady. The queue in front of me dwindles quickly until I'm next in line. The teller to the right of my Tiffany is serving a young woman in a business outfit. They almost complete their transaction. No, they're finished and I curse quietly to myself, shit. I tell the burly fellow behind me to go ahead. I pretend to search the contents of my wallet. "Where's my passbook," I whisper loud enough so that people can hear me, knowing full well that it is in the pocket inside my jacket. I look up and hear the elderly lady ask Tiffany what the difference is between interest compounded annually and that which is compounded semi-annually. I feel like I want to take a piss right now. I promise myself that from now on I will act on my feelings and if I do not act then I am nothing. And if I can't, then the world as we know it will end.

She smiles pleasantly when she's finished with the elderly lady. Here we go. I repeat silently the line that my favourite film is Ingmar Bergman's *The Seventh Seal*. Actually my favourite movie is *The Terminator* (the first one) starring the muscle builder, Arnold Schwartznegger, but I'm too flustered to gather my moral sensibilities together. I hate lying or even stretching the truth. My father is to be thanked for that.

I stand before Tiffany, both my hands clutching the withdrawal slip. She looks at me and a corner of her smile twitches nervously.

"And how are you today," she says.

"Very well. I'm excited about the film festival in The Annex next month." I pause to let her respond.

She glances at me as though she's puzzled at my remark but continues with her keypunching.

"They're screening *The Seventh Seal*," I continue nervously. "It's my favourite film."

"I haven't heard of that one before. Is it a Chinese or Japanese film?"

"No," I say, frustrated. "It's one of Ingmar Bergman's greatest, a masterpiece of European cinema." I enunciate emphatically the word *European*.

"Oh, you meant *The Seventh Seal*. I thought you said 'The Seventh Shield.'" She looks at me steadily. I start to say something but words run into a traffic jam in my dry mouth. "I didn't know European films are popular in Hong Kong," she says.

So what if this is the billionth time I'm mistaken for an immigrant, I console myself silently. I feel my scalp tightening. A headache is imminent.

After counting out my money to me, she delicately shoves the pile of bills towards me and smiles sincerely. She cocks her head slightly sideways as she does so. She says, "Have a good weekend, Mr. Chang."

"You too." I glance at her and notice her smiling lips crinkled slightly at the edges as if she senses something wrong with me. I say slowly, "You have a very good weekend." I say it very loudly, enunciating every syllable to ensure it is perfect English.

She forces a smile.

~~~

By the time I get into the elevator in my office tower, a dull headache throbs between my temples.

Back at the office everything seems to move so slowly. Fridays normally pass by quickly. Everyone wants to work harder and faster in order to finish their work sooner and get an edge on the rush hour traffic. Meanwhile, I sit back in my chair and watch the blue and white computer screen flicker in repetitive monotony. My 386XT computer is running a macro routine in a Lotus spreadsheet. Rows after rows of figures and names are created on the screen. The list seems endless, but eventually, maybe half an hour, maybe three hours later, the screen stops flickering. For that matter, it may have been an eternity or a mere tick of the clock. I write down the total figures and save the spreadsheet onto diskette. I regret staring too long at the flickering computer screen. My headache hurts even more. I regret not using the faster Pentium computer.

It is well past 4:30 PM and I poke my head above my cubicle. The entire floor is nearly deserted except for a few senior actuaries still in their offices, managing by example, I'm told. My supervisor, Bob Pickersgill, is still in his office. I can't see him from my cubicle, but I can hear the soft clicks of his computer keyboard. He's the only person in the office whose name we prefix with "Mister."

My hope for a quick escape is short-lived as I run face-on into Maureen Farquhar around the corner just as she finished filling her green mug from the water cooler. I bounce
~~~

off her chunky body but not before some water splashes on me.

"What's the big hurry, Lester? Got a hot date tonight?" She winks. Lately, she likes to tease me about my not having a girlfriend. She had never bought the idea I was "seeing" someone. For some uncanny reason she reads me better than even my own mother. Once when I told her I was seeing Wilma Fung off and on, she asked me if I like kissing Wilma. After some hesitation, I said, "sometimes." I knew then Maureen saw right through my game. She asked, "I bet you never even give her a peck on the cheek. Have you?" I whispered, "Only when I drop her off at the airport when she leaves town on business." After that I tried not to bullshit with Maureen and she's always been honest with me.

"It's past four thirty and it's Friday," I say.

"Quitting time, I know, but normally don't you work late on Fridays to earn brownie points with Mr. Pickersgill?"

"I don't know why but I'm pooped out right now."

"Same here. I'm just about to call it quits too." She drinks in one continuous gulp all the water in the mug, all the while keeping her eyes on me. Her thick glasses magnify her eyeballs so that I get the impression they may be billiard balls. Tufts of crinkled brown hair against the pale skin of her underarm suggest the hairdo of a Muppet. "Give me a couple of minutes and I'll walk you to the subway."

"Thanks, Maureen, but I really have to rush off." Right now, I don't feel like listening to her boyfriend problems which she has been dumping on me for quite a while now. No matter how the conversation starts out between us, it invariably ends up with her giving me a sob story on human relationships—*relationships* is a word I find too abstract for my liking but which she loves to use. For her, the idea of marriage, dating, courtship or even plain old fucking are subsumed under the grand umbrella of the word *relationships* as though she has discovered the holy grail of the meaning of life or the single formula uniting general relativity and quantum physics. And if it's not the sob story of her love life, it's a series of prophetic-like diatribes against the male species. She said once that I had a good nature and I would make a good priest if I were Catholic. Fortunately for me, I'm not.

"Who is she?" She smiles a child prankster's grin. There's very little that can faze me these days. Everything has become so banal for me. But she does have a knack for embarrassing people, mainly because nothing can embarrass her. "I've never seen such hustle in you to get out of the office so quickly. Who is the lucky woman?"

"Nobody," I say, trying to get around her.

She stands her ground, her hands on her hips. Tufts of brown hair peek out of her armpits. There's something about her that doesn't quite fit. It's as though she doesn't belong here in an office like ours working 8:30 to 4:30. The dull brown dress she's wearing reminds me of some costume made of chintz that might be used in a high school production of a medieval play. And then there's this laugh of hers which sounds like the laughter of a woman I once heard in the Queen Street Mental Health Unit when I visited an uncle there. It's a brief shriek that ends up in a giggle.

On better days, I seek her out for conversation. Being something of an outcast like myself, she's the only one I feel at ease with in the office. But not today, I don't want to listen to her sob stories. I've got to get out. My head ache is full blown now. Once she gets started, it'll be like last Friday when she went on for two hours about an international conspiracy to expunge any form of love from the world.

"I really have to get going, Maureen. We'll talk Monday."

She stretches her arms across the hallway like a man on a cross. I admire the smoothness of the white skin of her armpits, the gradual turning to white in the hollow of her underarm from the tan of the rest of her skin. Nice hairy arms too, she has, a thin carpet of golden hair on tanned forearms.

"Is that a promise, Lester?" She mocks a coyness in her voice.

"Sure."

"If we don't, you're a marked man."

"We'll talk over lunch," I promise.

Quietly and quickly, I slip out of the office, only nodding to the receptionist, a matronly figure sitting in front of her telephone console, reading some romantic novel.

The heat is still relentless outside. Into the underground malls and air conditioning I retreat. Down into the hollow of the earth where it is cool. There, with a bag of fresh popcorn in hand, I sit down on a beige marble bench and watch the world go by.

2

IT IS THE MOST ORDINARY of times between the seasons of birth and of death. Here, I stand in the humid summer air of a Toronto evening. Standing in my bachelor apartment, after hours of wandering the underground malls downtown, I'm lost as to what I ought to do next. Must I do anything at all? There is no disaster I must attend to, nor is there any passion that I am aware of.

My khaki-coloured suit is drenched in sweat. I sweat easily and profusely. I stare at the wounded skyline of the city along Lake Ontario. The sky is a deep, darkening blue. The CN Tower looks threatening, as if its sharply lit profile is about to gash the sky. At this moment in time, it stands blinking its flashes of light to ward off wandering planes overhead.

Then, the sound I have been dreading comes. It is much too late for those sounds, I tell myself. I look at the digital clock radio which sits mute and squat like a Buddha on an empty cardboard box in the corner of the room. It is only 7:53 PM. I have erred. I have thought it to be well past 9:00 PM. The ritual of dull thuds begins to sound from beyond the wall. I'm never sure where exactly the thumping comes from. It may be from the next door neighbour, a good looking red-head, who, I overheard from conversations she had with other tenants in the laundry room, is a stock broker. Or it may be coming from the unit just above mine. In any event, I only know that it comes from outside my one-room apartment.

As the thumping noise grows louder and more rhythmic, I feel a twinge of excitement replacing dread. I stand before the white gyprock walls like a monk before an altar. Now I hear voices. I can make out the female voice in strained cadence:

"Oh, my God. Oh, my God! Oh, Jesus Christ!"

Why is it that people cry out to God when they make love? I wonder if the Chinese cry out to God. Probably they do not because they do not believe in God. Not the majority of them anyway. They may cry out something like "Save me!" or "Save my life!" I think that's what was said in a life and death scene in one of the kung fu movies my father used to take us children to when we had just moved out to Toronto from our little town in Alberta eighteen years ago. That was one of his attempts at acculturating his children to Chinese culture after living among all those *fan gui lo*—barbarian ghosts—as my mother likes to call white men—in Spitting Hills, Alberta.

But I was never quite sure at the time what was said in those kung fu movies. The actors spoke Mandarin. Our family spoke a much different tongue, a dialect from Toisan County. I had this vague feeling that the English subtitles didn't quite match up to the dialogue. Or maybe it was just my general mistrust of the spoken word.

I don't ever remember hearing my parents make love. Even if I had heard, I might not have understood all the

Chinese words spoken. There were always words in the Toisan dialect that I had never understood but only felt and reacted to.

The phone rings but I ignore it. It is a rotary phone and its bell is jarring. I have often thought of getting one of those touch-tone sets with the electronic beep but I don't want to pay the extra $1.50 a month.

Actually, I hope the telephone ringing can drown out the muffled cries from beyond the wall. But the ringing stops and the thumping is even louder now. I see the leaves on the philodendron shake. The thought of my mind going crazy scares me. I remember once seeing little demons chomping away at my feet with razor-sharp-incisors. Later, I told myself that it was a dream when I was too young to think clearly. I no longer even believe that though. I suspect too much thinking is the real cause of my fears. Let me ask you: does a rock have nightmares? In any event, I'm happy to say that I no longer have nightmares.

Dropping to my knees, I press one ear against the wall in the hope of hearing the man's voice. Ever since this ritual began a few weeks ago, and every Friday thereafter, I have never heard a single word of a man spoken from across the wall during the thumping—some manly grunts, yes, but never articulated words. It was always the woman who spoke words. Sometimes it was, "No, Chris. No! Stop that!" On other occasions, it was "Faster, Chris! Harder, Chris!"

On swift tip-toes, I run to the kitchen and retrieve a glass tumbler. I remember seeing in some old movie how the hero used a glass for a stethoscope to amplify the sounds from a wall. But all I can hear when I get back to the wall is the hollow sound of the air between the gyprock.

The phone rings again. I answer it this time. It is my mother. We always speak to each other in the Toisan dialect.

She has never learned to speak English, except for a few phrases, despite living more than three decades in Canada.

"Lester. Why do you come home so late?" She says. "I have been calling since five o'clock."

"I come home when I feel like it. I'm a thirty-four year old man now, Ma."

"I don't care if you're one hundred years old. Until you're married you are still a boy. That's how the Chinese count it."

"Sure, Ma." I no longer try to argue over the phone with her any more, not since I left home seven years ago. It is so much easier to love your mother when you don't have to live with her. But whenever I'm back home for any reason, well, that's a different story entirely. I say, "So, what do you want to speak to me about?"

"Come home tonight and pick up your laundry, Lester."

Although I believe in being independent, I still like to keep ties with the family. And I know my father gets restless when he has nothing to do whenever my mother goes off to work for her Hong Kong employer at the noodle factory. He hates not working for a living. He doesn't know how to enjoy leisure, I guess. But in any event, no one is hiring old grill cooks anymore. So, I leave my dirty laundry with him every other week and pick it up whenever I need a fresh shirt or a pair of socks. He's quite good at keeping shirts unwrinkled, even better than Ma when she does it.

"I know, Ma. I didn't forget. I'll pick it up tomorrow," I say.

"Come home tonight. There is something very important I want to discuss with you, Lester."

"Yes, what is it?"

"It's about your father."

"So? What about him?"

"Be home tonight and I'll tell you."

"Why don't you tell me now?"

"I want to talk with you face to face. I have supper ready for you. I'm sure you haven't eaten yet."

"I was just about to go out for a quick bite." Actually, I have already eaten, but I'm getting hungry again.

"You've been eating out again, Lester? I told you to avoid greasy spoon cafes. You know we used to be in the cafe business and you ought to know how greasy and dirty a restaurant kitchen can be."

"I know. I know, Ma. I'll see you tomorrow."

"No, Lester, tonight. Why not just come home tonight for a bowl of ox tail soup. You need soup to counter the effects of all that fried food you've been eating."

"No, Ma! I'll drop over tomorrow." I slam down the receiver, feeling guilty immediately afterwards.

I have this insatiable urge for sweet and sour ribs on fried rice. I always want to stuff myself with fried foods after a conversation with my mother. I get this ringing in my head and an itch somewhere deep within me and I just have to head out for a bite. The gourmet burger I had earlier today in the mall just wasn't satisfying enough for me.

And I'm not even sure why I went into that gourmet hamburger restaurant at the mall in the first place. Maybe it was the possibility that it might serve the same kind of pure beef patties my father used to grill in our cafe back home in Spitting Hills, Alberta—seared on the outside to a thin crispness and juicy red on the inside. It was the seared beef scent which was most delightful about my father's burgers. What I got instead at the gourmet place was this overcooked, grey sponge served by this fellow with a little earring. Honestly though, I had hoped the tall blond woman would have served me, but it turned out she was not the waitress at all but the manager of the restaurant. With food, as with women, it is always its possibility of being more than what it appears to be that is its drawing power. It is not sex itself which makes women attractive, but the mere thought of having sex with them that excites me. So it is with food. I eat out, and often alone, hoping to recapture the flavours which were once so real to me in the past, a past which I once rejected to my regret and is no more.

What I savour most are not the trendy bistros or expensive restaurants in uptown Toronto, but those greasy grills along Queen Street, not the section transformed by the artsy crowd, but the dirty gaps in between the gentrified blocks where the patrons now pose with their glasses of Chardonnay.

Oh God, how I miss the scent of French fries cooked in lard.

Slowly but deliberately, I get out of my office suit and jump into the clothes which I have worn since university. There is no need to rush, I tell myself, when my objective is decided upon and clear: I will have a Chinese combination plate tonight.

There's only one place I've discovered in Toronto that makes sweet and sour ribs and beef fried rice the way my father used to make them. That's the Red Rose Cafe in the neighbourhood at the east end of Toronto known as The Beaches. In my estimation, it's a real find.

It's the culmination of a search that I had begun almost a year ago. I had been exploring any greasy grill cafe I could remember seeing in Toronto.

~~~

The neon sign of the Red Rose Cafe is a welcome sight for me. The dirty white paint is peeling in curls behind the neon
~~~

sign. One of the neon tubes is burnt out in the final letter "d" in the phrase "Good Food" to make it read "Good Fool."

Inside, Ken Wong, the owner who doubles as a waiter, greets me. "How are you, Buddy?" He calls all his men customers "Buddy" if he doesn't know their real names. The older women he calls "Lady" and the younger ones "Miss." I return his salutation with a "Fine, thank you. How are you?"

"Not very good. No rest for the wicked. No rest for the wicked."

I point to the two-seat booth near the back where I usually sit.

"Sure thing, Boss," he says. He likes calling me Boss or Captain when he's thinks I'm being arrogant. But tonight I'm not sure what I'm doing or wearing would suggest that to him.

He plops a tattered menu onto the table. Quickly, he gets me a cold glass of water, dripping wet along the sides. Simultaneously, he scatters a knife and a fork onto the table, not caring at all about the etiquette of table settings.

Even though I already know what I want, I still like to peruse the menu, looking for something familiar. Yes, breaded veal cutlets are the special tonight. My father used to cook the best veal cutlets, I believe, in all of Canada. He coated them in fine flour and bread crumbs, grilled to a crisp coating, and tender as though the meat is chicken. I wonder if the veal cutlets here can match my father's. But then again I still have this craving for sweet and sour and a mound of beef, no make that, mushroom fried rice.

That's the problem with living in the latter part of the twentieth century—too many options, too many choices and one must decide and act. Often I find myself paralysed by too many decisions. Take as an example, the ideal girlfriend: petite or strapping tall, reticent and demur or articulate and brash, soul mate or lusty lover, ad infinitum. The permutations are infinite. The endless possibilities suffocate my will.

One thing, however, is certain. I prefer, given a choice, white women. But lately, I have been reconsidering the possibility of settling for a Chinese girlfriend since I haven't been too lucky with white women. She must be English speaking and thoroughly Canadian. I would like a Chinese Canadian girl even more if she's bilingual—English and French, that is.

At least here at the Red Rose, I have the confidence that if I don't eat veal cutlets tonight, I can always eat them the next time I come back. Decision is made. I shall have the sweet and sour spareribs and mushroom fried rice combination. This combination is not on the menu but Ken and the other waiters give me a special deal on it. The price is the same as one of the regular combination plates listed on the menu, but they would ask the cook to heap an extra high mound of fried rice on my order. Ken always says, "Chinese eat rice."

When he sees me put down my menu, he quickly wobbles back to my table. He is the most deft and agile of the waiters at the Red Rose. He wears a white jacket as all the waiters do here. A salvo of pens and pencils are clipped on his jacket's breast pocket and another pencil usually is set at an angle on his ear. In my childhood memories, it seems all the Chinese Canadian cafes have their Chinese waiters wear white jackets. But now, I see them only in the Red Rose Cafe.

"Sweet and sour spareribs and beef fried rice tonight, Buddy?" He raises his cheeks a bit in anticipation.

"Not quite, I think I'll try the sweet and sour ribs with mushroom fried rice this time."

"Sure thing, Buddy. A little spice in life, eh, Buddy."

For some reason, clichés don't sound like clichés in this little man's mouth. The clichés are dead words resurrected, merely because he delights in saying them.

I slip two quarters into the jukebox and select Bob Dylan's "Mr. Tambourine Man." I always relish the line about following the Tambourine Man. Who do we follow now? Not God. Not the Prime Minister. Not father. Not mother. No one. I feel sad that even following my own heart has never gotten me anywhere.

But I cheer up quickly when Ken brings me my order. The sweet and sour ribs are always fresh on Friday evenings, and tonight is no exception. The deep-fried batter on the ribs retains its crunchy texture even when smothered in the sauce which has a soft orangey hue instead of the incandescent, magenta glow found in the sweet and sour spareribs of the other Chinese restaurants in Toronto. I alternate between munching a single piece of sweet and sour with a mouthful of fried rice.

As I savour my meal, I look up at the glass shelves of lemon meringue, coconut cream, apple, and to my surprise, Boston cream pies. It can't be, I think to myself. I haven't seen a Boston cream for ages. Half-way through my meal I ask Ken for a slice of Boston cream pie and a vanilla milkshake.

3

MY PARENTS LIVE IN A brown brick house within walking distance from Broadview and Gerrard, in an area which may be considered Toronto's third Chinatown after the older ones west of Yonge Street. Our house looks so small now. The wooden steps still creak as I mount them.

The neighbourhood was once predominantly working class and ethnic. Now increasing numbers of yuppy couples are buying up the old houses. Whenever I take a stroll in the old neighbourhood these days, I look through the new panoramic windows and notice newly renovated interiors of those homes. Sometimes, the living rooms are painted an off-white colour; peach is a popular colour. Green hanging plants creep out of thick macramé hanging pots. Ikea shelves of books grace the walls. Where there is a blank wall, some art deco photograph of some dead celebrity, like maybe Einstein, in black and white with some caption beneath the portrait, occupies one wall. Or sometimes, there may be a single delicately painted Oriental picture or an African mask hanging on the wall to signify the liberal mind of its occupants. A simple beauty is cast about the living rooms of these renovated houses.

The living rooms that are much more gaudy with statuettes of the three overfed Chinese male figures that represent gods and large screen televisions are very likely homes of Chinese from Hong Kong. If there are two lion statutes guarding the entrance to the house, then I'm certain the residents are from Hong Kong.

As usual, my mother opens the door before I even reach the doorbell. She appears to have some sort of telepathic power to foresee my coming.

The next door neighbour is sitting on his front porch and stares at us. He is Chinese with black eyes hard as ball bearings. He moved in about a year ago with his family from Hong Kong when our old neighbours, the Chans, bought a new house in Markham. Rumour has it that the new neighbour owns other property in Toronto. My parents and he aren't speaking to each other since the time his college age son started throwing cigarette butts into our yard. My mother often told me about the incident. She asked the kid to stop throwing butts onto our yard. When he wouldn't oblige, she said to the father next door, "We are all Chinese. Why can't we get along?" But his son tossed a cigarette butt onto our lawn like it was his own even as she was speaking.

"What took you so long?" My mother greets me.

The hallway beyond the stairs is dark because my father refuses to use any light bulbs over twenty-five watts for the corridors. Piles of old newspapers and old phone books line the hallway along with several cardboard boxes from the supermarket. I toss my runners on top of an array of shoes just inside the door.

"I stopped for a coffee at Tim Horton's."

"*Len hao*—you dinkhead. We have coffee at home." It

seems the women of my mother's generation from Toisan casually use words like *dinkhead* or *shit-piss* in the Toisan dialect. But if they ever catch their children using four-letter English profanities they'd threaten curses on them.

"But I like Tim Horton's coffee better."

"Coffee is coffee wherever you drink it."

The air is moist with the scent of steamed pork and soya sauce. There is the scent of green onions too. The air has a thick, oily feel to it but is not entirely unpleasant. It makes the house feel warm.

I sit down on the same chair I would always sit on when I used to live at home.

On the table are two tin pie-plates of steamed dumplings which look like crescent moons except that they are more grey and translucent with a rubbery texture. Those are among my favourites. I douse with soya sauce several dumplings on the tin plate. The pork meatball inside the dumpling bursts with savoury juices as I bite into one. It tastes better than it looks.

"You still haven't learned your manners, Lester."

"Sorry." I sheepishly accept a small plastic plate and a tiny sauce dish from my mother. I transfer some dumplings from the tin plate onto the plastic one. She pours a dollop of soya sauce into the sauce dish, and soon I'm wolfing down the dumplings again. There she stands like a chipmunk beside me, hands curled limply in front of her, fingertips together. Her nose and mouth still have gentle curves on them more like those of a child than of a woman in her late fifties.

"Better than at the restaurants," she says.

"Of course, Ma."

She walks in little steps like a girl over to the counter where she pours coffee into two mugs. The women in the noodle factory where she works on-call tease her that she has become Canadian because she prefers coffee to Chinese tea, she has told me.

She begins shovelling two teaspoons of sugar into my mug, the one with the Canadian centennial symbol on it. I quickly object, saying that I'm old enough to do it myself, and besides, I have stopped taking sugar with my coffee now. My mother sits next to me with her podgy elbows on the table watching me eat. "Better than the restaurants," she says a couple of times more and I nod approvingly. She gets up and turns quickly to the old gas stove and ladles up some ox tail soup. After sitting down once again, she briefly recounts the virtues of cooking at home: less greasy, cleaner, tastier, and no MSG. The last item is not quite true. She does use a smidgeon from time to time at the insistence of my father who recommends a pinch to blend the flavours in a dish. I realize old habits of operating a cafe are difficult for my father to break.

A glance at the clock shows me it is already past noon. My father should be home soon, after his morning stroll around Chinatown.

I ask my mother why she had made a big fuss about wanting to see me last night when she knew I regularly come home every second Saturday for my laundry. It starts her usual spiel. She's pleased that I'm finally working in a steady job but according to her estimation, I should have been married by now. If not, then I should be at least seeing some nice girl, preferably Chinese.

"When the right one comes I'll know, Ma."

"What about that nice Fung girl? Are you still seeing her?"

"We're good friends." I feel uneasy at the word *good* and cringe at *friends*. They smack of a lie.

"So what about her? Isn't she your girlfriend?"

"Just friends, Ma. Just friends."

"How friendly do you have to get in order to marry someone these days? Your father hadn't even seen me until he came to marry me."

That isn't quite accurate. My mother has a tendency towards hyperbole. My parents had met when they lived in neighbouring villages in Toisan, but now she can't remember the incident. My father could never forget it and even recognized her photograph when one of his cousins showed it to him in Canada. My father once told me all this.

"The reason why I wanted to talk to you," she says, "is to make sure you come to your father's 70th birthday next Friday."

"Ma, why didn't you just tell me that over the phone last night?"

"I just wanted to make sure you remembered."

"God, how can I forget? All you need to do is give me a brief phone call and I'll promise to be there."

"You don't like to come home, I know. You want to have nothing to do with us." My mother turns her eyes away from mine. She always looks away whenever she is upset with anyone in the family.

"That's not true, Ma. It's just that this is a busy week for me. Besides, I've been home to see you almost every other week the last couple of months."

"To have me or your father do your laundry."

"I told you I could have done my own laundry, but no, you and Pa insisted on doing it."

"Why don't you stay home for supper and spend some time with us?"

"Doing what? Stare at that stupid T.V. and watch your Hong Kong soap operas which even you don't fully understand."

"What do you do all by yourself? I can understand it if you are at least dating some nice girl."

"I've got things to do. I have my own life to live."

"Why don't you ever bring home a date for supper. Your father and I rarely ever meet any of the girls you've dated. Are you ashamed of us?"

"God, here we go again."

She lifts up her shoulders, taking in a deep breath before letting go an exaggerated sigh. Loud sighing is her way of telling the family what a martyr she is for putting up with us. She then says, "Your father's turning seventy and none of his children are married. Your sister is shacked up with this *fan gui lo*, and your younger brother is lucky not to catch some venereal disease."

"Please Ma, drop it. Just have some faith in your children."

I get up and place my hand on her shoulder and say, "Look Ma, just have a little faith in your kids. Julie's considering marrying Bruno. She told me so not too long ago." She pushes my hand off her shoulder.

"That useless female bag! I'd rather she be dead then marry that *fan gui lo*." She directs her anger at the floor by sharply nodding her head towards it.

"That's the problem with you Chinese. You're the biggest racists I've ever met. You live in the White Man's country and you think they're worse than shit!"

"I wouldn't mind it so much if she marries a white man with a steady job like your cousin Sylvia's husband. The white boy she married is a successful real estate agent. You know they just bought their second house in Markham. Two detached houses. Just think of that. That's not counting their summer cottage near Georgian Bay."

"Look Ma, Bruno's going to do well. It's just a matter of getting the breaks."

"The way Julie talks about him, you'd think he's a real movie star. And then, there's Dwayne."

"What about Dwayne?"

"He could never hold down a real job either. Hundreds of ideas to make his first million before he's thirty and he's already twenty-nine and lives in a rented attic in some stranger's house. Why can't he stay home and give me half the rent money? Or for that matter, he knows he can live at home for free if he wants."

"Nobody wants to live in their parents' house nowadays. People need their freedom to live their own lives, to learn from their mistakes."

"I knew your father should have been stricter with you. Just look at all of you. You'll die with no one to look after you. No family."

"Shit, Ma! We tried so hard to please you and Pa. We all tried so hard. None of us went out in high school just so we could help Pa run his dinky cafe. We never had real friends. Then all of us lived like monks going to university. We all graduated and got our degrees. We're all independent but that's not good enough for you."

She closes her eyes for a moment as though she is about to fall asleep. Then she says, "I appreciate what you did. It's not that I'm blind. It's just that I'm concerned for your welfare."

"We're doing fine, Ma. Just have a little more faith in us."

"I do, Lester. I do. It's all those relatives of ours." This time, her sigh tells me she means it sincerely. But I get even angrier, because she sighs as if she wants pity for us all.

"The hell with them. Fucking bastards!"

She draws her shoulders back when she hears the English word *fucking*. She says, "You know your father's orphaned. All your uncles and aunts look down on him. See him as some street urchin with a bowl asking the Chang clan for handouts."

"He was only a kid when Grandma adopted him in China. How can anyone despise an orphan? That stinks. Only the damn Chinese think that way."

"The fact is—they do."

"I say the hell with the assholes. We just live our own lives."

"All I'm asking is that you invite Wilma to your father's birthday celebration this coming Friday."

"I don't think she would come, but I'll ask."

"How could she not. This will be your father's 70th birthday and how often does a man celebrate his 70th birthday. Ideally, he should be surrounded by his grandchildren on that birthday."

"Okay, Ma, I'll do my best. It's just that Wilma's very busy at this time of the year. Something to do with the quarterly accounting at her company. It's very unlikely she'd have time this week."

"Just try, Lester. You showing up with a girl would really boost your father's morale. He'll have hope at least. I know you've been a good boy. You've been kind to your mother and father. We appreciate the money you give us each month. It makes us very happy. I'm only concerned that there's no one to look after you when you grow old."

"I'll do my best. Wilma's only a friend. No guarantees okay, Ma?"

The front door clicks open and slams shut rattling the frame of the house. My father appears like a ghost among the living, emaciated, and white hair so thin that it seems translucent. He stands at the threshold of the kitchen doorway, his slim frame teetering slightly. On his head is the oversized white baseball cap I had bought for him at Christmas. He had kept hinting that he'd wanted nothing but a Blue-Jays baseball cap to commemorate their second World Series Championship.

"Lester," my father says raising his voice slightly at the last syllable like a child not wanting to disturb adults.

"Pa," I say. "You look good in that cap. First time this year I remember seeing you in it."

"Oh, I have just been saving it for the summer. I didn't want to dirty it up during the winter and spring weather. How are you, Lester?"

"Ma's just reminding me about the big birthday bash next Friday."

"No big deal. How's work?"

My mother frowns but purses her lips in silence.

I say, "Oh, pretty much the same. It's busy but it's fairly routine now for the summer."

"I know I've asked you before but what exactly do you do?"

Then I give him the usual long spiel about pension consulting, how I take the figures provided by employers and by my company's actuaries and how I run computer printouts of present values of money to be paid by the pension plan in the future. My father nods his head as if he is thoroughly impressed.

"So what I mostly get in the mail is the Old Age Security not the Canada Pension Plan," my father says. I affirm that that is the case as I have done many times before, that the small self-employment earnings that he had paid to himself resulted in a correspondingly small amount of CPP credits. My father nods as if he understands. I do not remind him that his government cheque also includes the Guaranteed Income Supplement, because the last time I did, he became despondent when he realized that the GIS is a benefit for low income people. How can a former business man like himself qualify for a welfare benefit, he had lamented, too proud to swallow his pride.

"That means your Uncle Yuk Ching will be getting a full Canada Pension Plan benefit when he retires?" My father asks.

"Yeah, that's fairly close to the facts, something like 80% of full CPP, Pa. If he maintains full employment at the sawmill, at his current earnings and overtime, he will be getting a sizeable pension from the Canada Pension Plan. This is in addition to the Old Age Security benefit and company pension."

"The son of a bitch! Just off the boat and the Canadian government is kissing his ass."

"Well, it has been eleven years plus about twenty more years in the future at full employment; that's a substantial chunk of pension credits when he retires."

"The point is us old-timers took a lot of shit so that these guests from Hong Kong and mainland China can have it easy. We operated businesses and paid taxes to our government to support those lazy bums in plush jobs."

My mother closes her eyes and quietly sits at the end of the table.

"Oh, before I forget," I say and pull out my wallet and ten twenty-dollar bills. I offer the money to my father who shakes his head and holds out his palms to push the bills away. "Go ahead, yesterday was pay-day."

"You're sure now, son?"

"Of course."

"You have enough for your own expenses? You have a lot of overhead now with the new apartment and all?"

"Sure, Pa. I'm alright. Here, take it."

"If you insist. Thanks, son. Thank you." He gently folds

the money without counting and puts it in his front pocket. "I saw a sale on prime-rib roast at Loblaws this morning. I think I'll go back and buy a roast. I'll make a roast for us. How about that, Lester? You'll be home for prime-rib tonight? I'll make mash potato and gravy like when we ran the cafe. Smooth brown gravy. No one makes gravy as smooth as your father, eh?" Like most men from Canton province, he is proud to consider himself a better cook than the women folk.

"Right, no one makes gravy as good as yours, Pa."

My mother gets up and removes another tin plate of steamed dumplings from the big pot on the stove. "Here, for you, Pa," she says to my father. "These are hot."

My father turns again to me, "Will you be home tonight for prime-rib roast?"

"No, I won't be back tonight. I'm sort of busy."

"Well, that's alright. I'll save you some and also some for your brother and sister if they drop by this Wednesday."

"I have to get going now," I say.

"I have an idea, why not invite your girlfriend Wilma home Wednesday for a roast beef supper," my mother says. She raises her fingers to emphasize her request.

4

MONDAY MORNING AT WORK, I'M enjoying the absence of my boss. In the peace of my cubicle, I munch on a warm bagel and cream cheese from Druxy's, and drink a hot cup of coffee from Tim Horton's. The telephone beeps softly in my cubicle.

"A long-distance call from..." the electronic voice abruptly mutes and a human voice comes on the receiver briefly. "J.M. Walmsly." The electronic voice asks me if I will accept the long distance charges and then politely asks me to answer with either a "yes," or a "no."

I recognize the name as belonging to one of our lawyer clients who retain our firm to do actuarial calculations on the value of a pension as matrimonial property in divorce litigation. My supervisor had informed me earlier that Mr. Walmsly might be considering a settlement during recess in a divorce trial and would be phoning me this morning from some court house in Northern Ontario not yet serviced by cellular phones. I had promised him that I could come up with the figures by this morning.

Wagging my head like I'm some sort of big shot, my feet

"

on my desk, I say into the phone, "Yes." I drop my jaw like I see some of the vice-presidents do in our firm.

There is a pause and the electronic voice repeats the command to answer with a "yes" or a "no." Again with all the clarity I can muster, I answer, "Yes." The electronic voice comes on again repeating the command for the third time. My shirt clings to me in sweat. The hair on my scalp stands up. This is what Joe Carter must feel at the plate with three balls and two strikes against him. I answer more slowly and deliberately this time. The dial tone comes through the phone steady and clear. Shocked, I slump into my chair, my feet plopping onto the plastic carpet protector.

At the moment, I have a sickening feeling. I go to the men's room to throw water onto my face.

An hour later my boss, Bob Pickersgill, Mr. Pickersgill as we refer to him at the office, shows up at the office, returning from a successful meeting with new prospective clients. He has this swagger in his walk whenever his prospects become our clients. I can hear him whistling some Walt Disney tune. He pops his head into my cubicle.

"Did J.D. Walmsly phone for the figures this morning?" He is mocking the initials for their pretentiousness with exaggerated enunciations. As long as I have been at this firm, I can only remember Mr. Pickersgill telling the jokes; everybody else is supposed to laugh in his presence. Otherwise it's all business for Mr. Pickersgill, bred of the Protestant work ethic.

"Yes," I say, hesitantly.

"Good, and did you give him the figures?"

"No, the phone disconnected."

"Hmm. Didn't he try to phone later?"

"No."

He shakes his head like a Labrador dog coming out of a bath.

Another ten minutes later, he's back into my cubicle. His face is moist and red like it has just been scrubbed with a stiff steel brush. His thick eyebrows are knitted together to form one huge mess of an eyebrow.

"Give me the figures for the Walmsly file."

I hand him the printout. The figures don't satisfy him. He asks me to print out the present value figures for early retirement age fifty-five, before and after taxes. For some unnerving reason, he looks closely at me, inspecting me for some defect as I carry out his orders. His voice is tense. I go around the cubicle and withdraw a page from the central laser printer and inadvertently cut a finger on the paper before handing it to him.

Shortly, he returns with a hand on top of the divider and the other on his hip.

"That was Walmsly on the phone." His voice squeaks a bit like whenever he is upset. "You gather that, I suppose."

"Yeah."

"You know what he just told me?"

"No."

"Take a guess, Lester."

"No, I can't."

"He, J.D. Walmsly, probably the biggest divorce lawyer in Toronto, told me that I ought to teach my staff to speak proper English. Can you guess why he would say something like that, Lester?"

"No, I can't."

"Neither can I. I had always thought you spoke English fairly well. But obviously you still have problems with spoken English. How long have you been in Canada?"

"I was born here."

"In any event," he knits his bushy eyebrows again. "Here's what I'm proposing to do. I know this excellent clinical psychologist who has on staff a speech therapist. I will be sending you and Clarissa to her for a few weeks to improve your English."

"Yeah?"

"The company will pay for it. I will throw in dinner and cab fare as well. I just don't want to lose my divorce clientele that I've been building up for the last five years. The Walmsly account is almost half of our divorce business and I don't need any kind of publicity detrimental to our firm."

Hanging my head low, I look at the frayed edges of the green blotter on my desk.

The thought of Clarissa Woo and I lumped together nauseates me to no end. I can bear with the idea that we may both look Chinese. And I still can hold on to the hard fact that she's from Hong Kong and I'm from the Canadian prairies. How can you change the colour of your skin, my mother would always admonish me whenever I say I am Canadian first. But to sound Chinese? I begin to sweat even though the office is air conditioned.

5

THE AUDIENCE IS SMALL AT tonight's screening of *Romeo Is Bleeding* at the theatre across from the Red Rose Cafe.

In the aisle seat fourth row from the front sits a woman with a halo of blond hair. She wears a beige halter top so that she appears naked from the back at first glance. She looks familiar.

I take my seat in the row immediately behind her, one seat to her right. There is a scent of peach herbal shampoo about her. I recognize something of baby powder as well.

I've come to see this movie for the third time mainly because of Lena Olin who stars in the role of a Russian criminal out to destroy the Gary Oldman character and the local gangster boss, but not before she screws them both. That's what I want too, sex before I die, open throttled, undiluted lust. I wonder if sex is best just before committing suicide. I suspect it may be, because there are two things that preoccupied my mind as a youth, and they were death and masochistic sex.

The incident earlier this morning with the electronic voice has drained me terribly, and all I want to do is watch

Gary Oldman under the thumb of Lena Olin, so to speak. My needs are simple and expectations reasonable. I pat my pocket for my wallet, confident that in a few hours I'll be happily jerking off into that condom, imagining Lena Olin on top of me like a cowgirl bucking a bronco.

Quietly, I sit in awe in the darkness of the theatre while people behind me munch on buttered popcorn, and on the silver screen, Lena Olin removes her pinstripe jacket. Gary Oldman is handcuffed to a brass bed, arms spread out, helpless as she straddles him. He is at her mercy. She can inflict her choice of exquisite torture on him. After she removes her jacket she is naked except for a pair of panties and a leather harness which leaves her breasts exposed. This would be the perfect torture scene had she stripped him of his shirt and had she commenced whipping him. But she does neither. The scene is something of a let-down. They only make love and even that is only suggested when she removes her leather harness which turns out to be holding in place an artificial limb.

As the final credits roll onto the screen and the lights slowly come on, I sit motionless, staring at the screen, mulling over this thought: the story context which gives most potency to the sex act is one of torture. This is where the twin threads of death and sex are drawn together.

In front of me, the woman with the golden halo stretches her arms and yawns. I admire the smooth hollow of her armpits. There is a tiny pimple on the white smooth of skin at the bottom of the hollow.

She turns her head to look across the theatre. I see her profile. It is Tiffany.

My impulse is to flee. I don't want another conversation with her. I'll stutter and flounder and confirm to her the mistaken image of me as a Chinese immigrant.

Why is it that I have these urges to be humiliated by a naked white woman in the privacy of a hotel room, but I'm devastated when I'm mistaken for a Chinese immigrant? I relish the thought of a leather belt whipping across my nipples while a white woman calls me Chink, but I'm embarrassed when even a nuance, a pause or a stare, suggests I'm more Chinese than Canadian.

Tired, droopy eyed, she appears like she just got out of bed. Her lips are pale without any lipstick. But their gentle curve is lovely. Pushing myself beyond fear, I say, "Do you work at the bank on the corner of King and Bay?"

"Oh, yes. Do I know you?"

"I'm one of your clients at the bank."

"I don't seem to remember. There're so many in that branch. In and out, hundreds every day. Hundreds."

"Lester Chang. I usually cash my pay cheque at your branch. Remember?"

"Oh yes. You're the fellow who's into Japanese films. Aren't you?"

"No, that's not me."

"I swear it was you who had an interest in *The Seven Samurais*."

"No, it was *The Seventh Seal*."

"Oh, yes. Now I remember. You're the Bergman fan." Her mouth twitches in recognition. So you're the guy who gave me a hard time, she's probably thinking. But God, she does look beautiful with her arched upper lip. The arc is a sign of her incredulity.

"Actually, I'm much more of a fan of Carl Dreyer, Bergman's predecessor and major influence."

"I wasn't aware of that. Who is Carl Dreyer?"

Here's my chance to impress her, I think. I'll lay it on thick to let her know my influences were Western, not Chinese. I say, "He is without doubt Denmark's greatest film director. In my mind, he is probably the greatest director who ever lived. The whole witch burning scene in *The Seventh Seal* is a copy of a scene from Dreyer's earlier film *Day of Wrath*, his critique of the seventeenth century Reformation church. His major themes appear to be religious. Church versus State. Divine revelation versus official theology. Personal religious experience versus church doctrine. God, I get an orgasm when I watch his films." I can't believe I said that.

"Really?" Her look of incredulity turns to one of uptightness. Her eyes dart about like an animal wanting to escape.

I panic. "But you know who his influence was?"

"Whose influence? Who are you taking about?" She appears to be getting a hold of herself again. She's once again in the driver's seat.

"Dreyer's influence. It was Søren Kierkegaard."

"Oh." Her lips quickly tighten. She's lovely when she's angry. "The father of existentialism." She is smug.

"Yeah. But he was really a believer in orthodox Christianity. You might even say Kierkegaard was a sort of closet, born-again-Christian."

The street is nearly empty of people. The lights from the theatre are out. In the far distance, a street car rumbles. Along the horizon, the CN Tower blinks. Here I stand at the intersection of two streets in Toronto on a clear summer night that is indistinguishable from any other clear summer night. I want to make a connection with the past and with the girl in front of me by dropping a litany of names, Bergman, Dreyer, Kierkegaard, that somehow I can become more intimate with her by resurrecting the ancestors of her past.

"But isn't existentialism atheistic?" She says.

"Their modern devotees may be, but Kierkegaard, who, by the way, never coined the word *existentialism* himself, was in fact writing from an ironic posture when he attacked Christendom."

"That's all very interesting, but it is getting late and I have to work tomorrow."

Shit, I'm losing her. I have to say something more engaging. "The thing I like about Kierkegaard most is his emphasis of the particular over the general. Besides the corruption of the nineteenth century church, he was concerned with the scientific and objective point of view invading the personal aspect of faith."

"I really have to get going." Her arched lip is wonderfully beautiful.

"You see, he once wrote that faith has become secretly embarrassed and ashamed like a young woman whose lover, in and of himself, is no longer sufficient for her. She needs to prove to herself that there is something remarkable about him before she can love him. She can no longer love her lover just as he is."

Tiffany takes a step back. Then she turns to walk away.

Not knowing what else to say, I raise my hand to wave good bye although she already has her back to me. I watch her go up one of the residential streets. She leaves me standing on the street corner trying to figure out what has just transpired.

6

"is that your hot date, Lester?"

I'm startled by the smokey voice which sounds like someone who's hoarse from screaming. There's a scent about her I can't quite place, something like rancid butter, mingled with a waft of booze. It's Maureen Farquhar from my office. "Oh, hi there, Maureen." There's a wimpiness I notice in my own voice.

"You haven't answered me, Lester. Is that blond bombshell your date?"

"Well, not exactly."

"You're still being vague. She's not your date, is she now?"

"No. She's someone I met at the theatre."

"You know what, Lester?"

"What?"

"I'm glad you're honest and open with me. Sincerity is one of the things I like in a man." She pauses to collect her thoughts. "I was sitting a couple of rows behind you in the movie theatre. You were alone. I was watching."

"I didn't know you like watching Gary Oldman films?"

"I don't. Something to do. Something to fill the loneliness."

Maureen tends to be blunt, but normally her bluntness is tempered with humour. Tonight her frankness has a brutality about it. There's a yearning in her voice which eludes me at the moment.

"Matt's a week overdue for his 'conjugal' visit," she says as a matter of fact. "I don't think he's coming back this time."

She's referring to her ex-boyfriend's monthly visits with her for sex. It's her last hint of hope for what she thinks is love.

"I've tried phoning him and all I get is his answering machine for the past week. He's not answering my messages at all. What am I to do, Lester?"

Why ask me? What do I know about love when I'm just asking for a little more than lust? But I'm not entirely surprised though that she asked me for answers to mend her heartbreak. Sharing her intimate secrets with me has become routine at the office. We've become confessor and confessant. I should have been a priest, she says. But I am coming to enjoy my role. I suspect I know more about her than even her own boyfriend, I mean, ex-boyfriend.

I invite her to join me for coffee at the Red Rose Cafe. She can dump her worries on me. I feel like a martyr right now. Nothing better for your own woes than to help others with theirs.

Inside the Red Rose Cafe, Ken sees me walking to my usual booth. He says, "Hello, Buddy! How are you tonight?"

"Hi, Ken," I say. I look at Maureen. "Two menus?" She doesn't respond, staring blankly at the table. I nod to Ken to bring the menus. Meanwhile, I ask him for two coffees.

Maureen suddenly becomes aware of her surroundings. "Do you have tea? Herbal tea, do you have any herbal tea?"

"Sorry, Miss. Just regular tea. Orange Pekoe."

"That'll do." As Ken turns to get the order, she says, "I'd

like some lemon with that. Make that lemon and honey, please."

"Sure thing, Miss." Ken looks slightly annoyed but takes her behaviour as a matter of course. Perhaps, moviegoers from the theatre across the street tend to be depressed or angry when they come into his cafe.

Now in the bright fluorescent lights of the cafe, I see that her eyes are blood-shot.

"You look miserable, Maureen. You look the shits if you want my honest opinion."

She cracks a smile, more of a smirk than a simple smile, but a smile nonetheless. With her Prince Val style hair dishevelled, she is like a thirty-five year old tom boy. And if the crow's feet had disappeared from her soft face, I'd swear she was a youngster who just finished bawling. Taking off her black rimmed glasses, she just sits there with her lips puckering into an O. It's hard to believe she can sit still and be silent.

After browsing the menu and still can't make up my mind what to order, I happen to look up and see the banana-shaped handles of two taps for dispensing carbonated water used in making fountain cokes just like the ones served in my family's first restaurant. The Red Rose Cafe is the only restaurant in Toronto that still serves an old fashion fountain coke. I like to watch Ken squirt the dark syrup over the chipped ice in a soda glass, fill it with carbonated water, mix, and finally stick two straws into the concoction. I really believe a fountain coke tastes better than coke out of a can or bottle. There seems to be something liturgical about the preparation of the drink. I decide then to order a fountain coke in a tall soda glass and a large plate of fries and gravy. Maureen refuses my offer to buy her a snack. She's not hungry, she says.

While we wait for my order, I'm getting a bit anxious just sitting there. We look forty-five degrees away from direct eye contact. Elbow on the table, she leans her face against the palm of her hand and distorts her cheeks and lips in a school girl sort of way. I am glad when the fries and gravy arrive, so that there's no need to feel like I have to carry on a conversation. "Want some?" I ask her. She shakes her head, no. She watches me eat.

Picking up a French fry dripping with brown gravy, I gingerly lick it. The fries are too hot to eat right away, so I let them cool off for a little while. Fortunately, Ken brings over the fountain coke, so I can drink a mouthful of it and let it linger in my mouth for a while.

Maureen gives me this look that is like the ones elementary school girls used to give me when I was a kid. "You're weird, Chang," they used to say to my face. I sort of liked that attention. Actually, I find Maureen's incredulous look appealing, brow furrowed and mouth pouted. With much gusto, I begin eating my fries again, cooling bite-size pieces in my mouth with gulps of coke.

"You really take eating seriously, don't you, Lester?"

"Sure do." I pretend to be like those cowboys who don't give a damn what people think of them, sort of like the cowpoke who plays opposite Marilyn Monroe in the movie *Bus Stop*. "Aaah," I sigh and snap my head a quarter turn. "*Wunderbar.*"

"You look silly eating like some country hick." She helps herself to a French fry.

"Hey, I thought you're not hungry, kid."

"I changed my mind." She helps herself to more of my fries.

"I'll order another plate."

"No. That's fine."

I raise my hand to order and she slaps it down. She does it in jest. But she goes on eating the fries as we talk until they're all gone.

After a slight pause to inhale a breath, she says, "I appreciate you spending time with me, Lester, not just now, but at the office, having lunch with me, letting me bend your ears."

I smile, not knowing what to say.

She goes on, "I don't get it. I just don't understand why I'm always stuck with the assholes of the world for boyfriends." She purses her lips as if to stop the flow of tears welling up in her eyes. After she blows her nose, it looks redder and it has a life of its own as it widens and tightens at will. It reminds me of Dianne Keaton's nose. She says, "All I want is love and a little respect. Is that asking too much?"

Feeling helpless and awkward, I order another plate of fries and gravy.

She says, "Do you see what I mean, Lester?"

"I think so."

"I knew you would understand. Nobody else does." She starts heaving her shoulders up and down, unable to control her tears this time. Instinctively, I extend my hand across the table and hold hers. She squeezes mine tightly.

A few of the night-time customers stare at us. I like it. Maybe they think we're lovers. I really don't entertain any serious affection for this poor thing, but she's not exactly a dog, now, is she? It's a cute game to play and I don't feel uncomfortable now as I think about people's perception of us, a Chinese guy with a white gal. The Chinese might see her as a *lo fan*—a derogatory term in Chinese for a white person, but she's my *lo fan* girl. I brush my thumb gently across the back of her hand.

Ken stops at our table with an armful of orders, three hamburger platters stacked in one hand, a Chinese combination plate cradled on the crook of that same arm and a plate of fish and chips in the other hand. He says to Maureen, "He good man. Only problem, he eat too much."

She laughs, watching him from the top of her eyeballs, as Ken saunters off with his orders to another table, shuffling his feet like Charlie Chaplin doing the 100 yard dash.

"Is it true that all men think about is sex?"

I nearly choke on my fountain coke, some of it running up my nose. "Eh, I don't really know."

"You mean you don't ever get aroused?"

"Of course I do. I mean...."

A pause before Maureen continues talking.

"I'm sorry to put you on the spot, to tease you so," she says.

"Apology accepted."

"You're so easy to tease. You don't take things so seriously like everybody else at the office. You can take jokes. Those are the things I like about you. Let me put the question to you another way. Don't you think one ought to love the person above all else?"

"Person? What do you mean, Maureen?" I can't bear to look at her intense watery eyes, so warm in their hazel colour. It's as though I'm afraid they will dissolve through my lewdness, my own prurient thoughts.

"Don't you think the most important thing about your lover...?"

"I don't have one right now."

"Suppose you do. Don't you think the most important aspect about her would be her inner beauty?"

"Inner beauty?" What novels has she been reading? Maybe she knows Barbara Cartland? This is not Maureen talking, is it? Maureen who can keep pace with the boys' profanity at the office, Maureen with the hairy but lovely armpits?

"Yes, Lester, what counts in a lover is what she is like on the inside."

7

NEXT DAY, TUESDAY AT LUNCHTIME, Wilma and I agree to meet for lunch in the lobby immediately behind the revolving doors of the Eaton Centre. Doing lunch with her has become a sort of ritual that comes and goes in spurts ever since Wilma got me that job in the pension consulting business, almost seven years ago, shortly after she had become a Fellow of the Society of Actuaries.

As I wait for her, I ponder over how I have come to like her little androgynous figure, her heart shaped bum in particular.

I don't recall when or exactly how we got to know each other. I think it was in a first year calculus course. There she was, right in front of me, sitting almost beneath my very nose. She was one of those people who would get invited to a party and nobody there would notice whether or not she had arrived. Even during those undergraduate years, she wore that short haircut. With simple bangs across the forehead and tapered side-locks, she reminded me of an elf.

Wilma is standing in the Eaton Centre lobby near the metal railings. She seems to have popped out of nowhere among the crowd. One moment, a crowd of strangers mill-ing about the rotunda, and the next, this female elf walking towards me and then abruptly stops to wave at me. The face is irrefutably Wilma's, undistinguished, except her lips which are always in a pose as though they are about to ask a question. She waves splayed fingers mechanically at me.

"Hi there." Her voice doesn't sound authoritative as a vice-president ought to sound. Instead, it sounds like her words are curled by one of those old fashion telephone operators in a 1940s movie, somewhat nasalized. "You've been waiting long?"

"Nope. Just got here."

I compliment her on her new dress, a white one with huge roses in blue, red or yellow, the length of it reaching her calves. Mincing her lips just slightly, she looks embarrassed. Over the years, I've mentioned to her that she looks good in a dress, but she usually prefers wearing pants.

It dawns on me that I find it very easy to speak openly with her, laying on the compliments as well as less flatter-ing though honest opinions about her appearance, an ease which I seldom have around far more attractive women. Being around this impish figure is relaxing, like being with the boys for a round of beer.

We begin as always with Wilma letting me choose the restaurant and end up invariably in one which I detest but she likes. I suggest the H&M Cafe, the greasy grill just off Queen Street. She replies by quoting statistics correlating animal fat and cancer of the colon. Then I argue that city-by-laws forbid any restaurant to use animal fat anymore, but she quotes figures about E-coli bacterial count on improperly cooked hamburgers.

Finally, we settle on going to the Marine View Room, a fancy cafeteria, on the department store's top floor.

As usual, there are hordes of little old ladies milling about and having their lunch at tables as close to the windows as possible.

At the hot entrée counter, I order the meat loaf special which has the texture of canned Spam. But I like Spam.

Meanwhile, Wilma orders a grilled cheese sandwich, fruit salad and coffee. At the grill counter, I wait for her as she waits for her order to be cooked.

"What are you standing around for?" She says.

"Waiting for you."

"Your meal is getting cold."

"I don't mind. I'll eat anything as long as it doesn't move."

She rolls her eyes up and around. The corners of her mouth dip down. We wait for the order in silence.

Together we walk up to the cash registers each holding our plastic trays gingerly like monks in a breadline, individually alone, but strung together with a thin, invisible thread.

"There's a cashier available at the far end over there. Why don't you take it?" She nods her head towards the clerk with the sleepy eyes at the far end.

"That's alright. No rush."

She rolls her eyes again and purses her lips like when she's frustrated. I had intended to buy her lunch in light of her new promotion, but think better of it.

As she pays her bill I peer down the nape of her thin neck. A Chinese Audrey Hepburn from the back, I think to myself. Yes, thin, white and long is her neck. There's a peachy, fresh scent about her today. She's using an herbal shampoo, I'm sure of that.

At a table in the dark corner of the room we have our meal. We don't say anything until she breaks the silence.

"How's your meat loaf?" She studies me.

"Good. How's your sandwich?"

"The bread's stale. The fruit salad tastes fresh, though."

"Too bad about the sandwich," I say and put down my fork and knife in order to make like I'm gathering my thoughts, elbows on the table and hands under my chin.

"What's the matter, Lester?"

"I just want to congratulate you on your promotion at Sterling Global."

"Thanks." She smiles gently. There's no empty arrogance about this girl: just a calm confidence in her as she chews each mouthful of fruit salad slowly and deliberately. And that's what is so scary about her. She has this confidence and self-assurance about her that if she has a conviction that you're an asshole then all the stars in heaven will be on her side, confirming that you're an asshole.

"How long have you known about it?"

"What did you say, Lester? Speak up. I can't hear what you're saying."

I dredge up as much phlegm as possible in my dry throat and make like I'm clearing my throat. "When did you first know about your promotion?" I enunciate each individual word slowly and deliberately.

"A month and half ago." She then stiffens her lips. Her smile is gone. Her eyes move up and down, studying me once again.

"I don't think that you ever mentioned about your promotion to me."

"You thought correctly." She's obviously enjoying her fruit salad as she carefully dredges her bowl for the last bit of fruit.

"Why didn't you?"

"Didn't what, Lester? What didn't I do? You ought to complete your sentences, Lester. Nobody's going to understand what you're saying."

I want to pick her up by her beautiful neck and shake her

up against the wall. And I don't know what's coming over me, this frustration at not being understood in plain English.

"Why didn't you tell me that you were getting a promotion?"

"It's nothing to get excited about."

"Nothing to get excited about? Becoming vice-president and chief actuary in one of the top ten life insurance companies in Canada is something to celebrate."

She shrugs her shoulders. "Anyway, now you know."

"And about a million readers across the country knew before I stumbled onto your photo in the *Globe and Mail*."

"I didn't know you read the *Globe and Mail*, Lester?"

"Of course I do. What makes you think I don't? It's the only local paper that gives me all the stock prices as of Friday closing."

"Still gambling in the VSE crap-shoot, Lester?"

We avoid eye-contact for a while. I stare at the outline of her collar bone. There's a dark brown spot on her neck I never noticed before. Its edge seems vague like the penumbra of a lunar eclipse. I conclude it's a birthmark.

"I was wondering if we can start getting together again for supper once a week like we used to," I say.

"You mean once a week for take-out barbecue chicken?"

I used to drop by her place for rotisserie chicken from Swiss Chalet each week. It started when we celebrated my first full-time job, the one she recommended I take seven years ago. She had wanted to treat me to anything I wanted. I had a craving for Kentucky Fried Chicken at the time. She thought it was too greasy for her digestion and we compromised on rotisserie chicken from Swiss Chalet. Somehow it became sort of a ritual from then onward, having Swiss Chalet chicken at her place weekly.

We tried home cooking at one point, but she wasn't a

good cook and I was worse. Instant noodles in beef bouillon, heavy on the Tabasco sauce, were her specialty. So, we agreed to continue taking turns ordering Swiss Chalet chicken. It was only a couple of years ago that we stopped having our weekly chicken dinners after we "broke up."

I say, "Sure. We can do that again. But what I have in mind this Friday is supper with my parents."

"What?"

"I mean if you're free."

"What if I am free, why are your parents having me over for supper? I've only met them a couple of times. I don't really know them."

"That's just the point. I'd like to have you over just for an evening in order to get to know them better. You'd like them, once you get to know them."

Her lips stiffen as she gathers a breath. She says, "No, I don't think it's a good idea."

"Why not? It'll just be an evening with friends."

"No."

"Why not, Wilma?"

"Because, Lester, it just looks too much like a boy taking his girlfriend home to meet his parents. Let me make this very clear. You and I are friends. Not girlfriend. Not boyfriend. Just friends. Don't you see how easy it would be for people, especially Chinese people, to get the wrong idea that we're serious about each other?"

I find it difficult to breathe. My chest is chilling like a blast of cold wind across a glacier.

"Something is bothering you, Lester?" She says.

"I'm sorry. I was thinking that there's nothing wrong with having you over for my father's 70th birthday party as my guest. A friend."

"I don't know, Lester. Will all your family and relatives be there?"

"Yeah, sure. Most of them will be there. Don't worry about them."

"The Chinese take those 70th birthdays fairly seriously. And besides, I find Chinese gatherings tedious and full of dangerous gossip."

"Like I said, don't worry. It's over between you and me. We'll always just be friends. I promise. I'll make it clear that we're not an item at the party."

"What do you mean over? What is there to be over? Explain yourself, Lester."

"I know how much our relationship had once meant to you."

"Relationship? Like in boyfriend, girlfriend sort of relationship?" She contorts her lips at the word *relationship*.

"Yes, exactly."

"Whatever gave you such a silly idea?" She looks sincerely puzzled. "God, you've been inside your head for too long, Lester. I'm surprised. I've always thought we were just friends."

"We did see each other fairly regularly once." And for good measure, I add, "And good friends share their triumphs."

"Triumphs?" She shakes her head like a little poodle coming out of a bath. "You funny boy. Which planet did you come from? I never thought of you as a boyfriend if that's what you mean. I'm shocked. Having barbecue chicken together once a week doesn't make us lovers."

8

WEDNESDAY MORNING, I GET OUT of bed early, because I haven't been able to sleep a wink. I figure if I just get through the day I'll be okay.

As soon as I get out of the subway station, I head straight for the H&M Cafe, hoping to eat a hearty breakfast of bacon and eggs, eggs over easy, and a stack of white toast, and of course, that wonderfully brewed coffee. Now I can appreciate how grateful the customers of my father's cafe in the prairies must have been for his presence. The farmers coming to town on business, the milkman, the postman, even the mayor on occasions, and many others, single men, married men, all lonely men, they all came and sat at my father's cafe in Alberta and lost themselves in conversation with Wai Chang, or simply the Chinaman, as some of the older men might have affectionately referred to him. But they all appreciated his ear, listening to their problems or simply listening to their bullshit. The fact that he probably didn't understand half of what they said didn't matter. What did matter was that another human being was standing there as they muttered and babbled about life.

When I get to the H&M Cafe, it is closed. Something out of the ordinary has happened. The old Chinese couple has decided to take life a little bit easier. The crayon scrawled sign says they are opening now at 11:00 instead of 7:00 in the morning. Yes, they are getting old. They are about the same age as my own parents but a lot more spry.

But I'm disappointed.

I go back underground into the malls branching off from the subway entrance. I spot a tea and coffee specialty shop not too far from my office. There's nothing grungy about this upscale setting. It is so clean that I doubt even a microbe would want to live there. But that'll do for now. I just need a cup of freshly brewed coffee.

A pale faced Chinese woman in her early thirties is overseeing the cash register. Her dry black hair is pulled back tightly in a bushy ponytail. I suppose she might even be considered good looking had she put on a bit of makeup. Even just a bit of lipstick would take away some of that drudgery from her face.

I ask her if she serve bacon and eggs, even though I suspect the trendy setting doesn't suggest anything greasier than healthy muffins. When she answers no, I ask for a carrot muffin for no particular reason other than having seen a row of them right in front of me.

I'm glad just to sit down and drink my coffee out of a large styrofoam cup. The red and turquoise embossing on the cup appears extremely complex, a detailed abstraction that makes me feel uncomfortable. I try not to look at it again. I hold the cup between my hands the way a priest might gingerly guard a silver chalice in the Eucharist.

The coffee is bitter and I regret not walking the extra couple of blocks to the Tim Horton's Donut shop.

The muffin tastes burnt. And I know why as I listen in

on the dialogue between the Chinese woman with the dry hair and one of her employees, a young Chinese man.

She is giving him a tongue lashing in loud Cantonese. The language is so simple and straight forward that even I can understand it.

"Do you know what you just did to me," she asks the young man who now hangs his head, averting his eyes from hers, while she searches his face. When he doesn't answer her, she says, "You just threw away eighteen dollars. Every single one of these muffins is burnt."

"I'm sorry," the young man says.

"Not only did you manage to throw away eighteen dollars, but I pay you seven dollars an hour to bake that batch of muffins. Does it make any sense that I should be paying you to waste time and to throw away my profits?"

Before she can finish her tongue lashing, a customer comes to the cash counter. He's a tall, handsome fellow in blue pinstripes. They exchange greetings on a first name basis. They chit-chat like old friends. Her accent is that of someone from Singapore where English is an official language. She is very articulate in discussing the impact of a separatist Quebec. After the customer receives his order and goes to a table, she turns back to her employee who has been standing silently beside her like a faithful servant. She repeats what she has said earlier, reminding him of her loss and his shame.

"Is that how you guys work in China? No wonder the Communists had to shoot a few of you," she finally says. I sense in her pause that she knows what she has just said is a gaffe. But she quickly shakes off any guilt about hurting the young man's feelings.

The young man's face flushes red and moist, but after that he is emotionless.

I sit at my little table and watch the flow of people from the subway gradually increase. Soon the sounds of individual clicking of heels on marble become one massive drone and the individual human voices become a monotony of white noise. I get up and head for my office.

~~~

On my desk is a yellow memo note from Mr. Pickersgill summoning me to go to his office as soon as I come in. He signs it in his abbreviated signature "RKP" in large flourishes.

His office is as messy as ever. Stacks of computer print-outs are strewn everywhere. Sitting behind a huge desk at least three times the size of mine is a relaxed Mr. Pickersgill, hands clasped behind his head. To his right is Clarissa Woo in a pink dress.

"Come on in, Lester," he greets me cheerfully. "We're just discussing plans about your sessions with the speech therapist I've mentioned to you on Monday."

"Oh, yeah, the English lessons," I mumble.

"Clarissa has a fairly packed schedule," he says and then swings his chair around slightly to face her. "Don't you, Clarissa? I believe you said that only Wednesday is free for you to go to those speech therapy sessions?"

She nods to him and then smiles a creepy smile at me.

"Well, discuss it between yourselves and get back to me when you both decide on a day to meet weekly, so I can get back to Mrs. Shannon Fay, the speech therapist, on this."

"Mr. Pickersgill, I prefer not to make it on Wednesdays," I say.

"It's a matter for you to discuss with Clarissa. Just let me know when you two agree on a day."
~~~

"I'm firm about Wednesdays. I plan to schedule my study days on Wednesdays."

"Oh, you've decided to write some actuarial exams this fall, Lester? I thought you wanted to take a break."

"I changed my mind, Mr. Pickersgill."

"Good for you, Lester. I'm glad to hear that."

"Mr. Pickersgill," Clarissa says, "I too am firm about Wednesdays. My eldest daughter's piano lessons is on Tuesdays and her ballet lesson is on Thursdays. And Fridays are both my daughters' Chinese lessons after school. I've got to be out of here on time to pick them up from public school. I only have Wednesdays free for this speech therapy thing."

"Like, I said, it's a matter to work out between you two," Mr. Pickersgill says in a huff, annoyed at our fickleness.

"I'm sorry, Mr. Pickersgill, I'm set about Wednesday," I say.

"So am I," Clarissa says.

"Can't you make arrangements with your nanny, Clarissa?" Mr. Pickersgill asks her in a friendly voice. "I'm sure she'd be flexible about that."

"She still doesn't have her driver's license yet."

"What about Mondays?"

"I have to be home early on Mondays because my nanny has her prayer meetings on Mondays and needs to leave early."

Clarissa stares at me with ball-bearing eyes.

I say, "I'm sorry, Mr. Pickersgill, I guess we'll have to cancel the whole business about the English lessons."

Now Mr. Pickersgill turns to glare at me with his dark brown eyes.

"What did you say?" He says, squeaking a bit at the end of the sentence. "Are you refusing my request to improve your communication skills, Lester?"

"If you want my honest opinion, I think all this is a waste of time," I say, feeling bold.

"Are you defying a direct order from me, Lester?" His voice breaks again. This is the old Mr. Pickersgill coming through, the one I once so feared.

"No," I half-whisper.

"What did you say? Speak up. I can't hear what you're saying."

"No, sir."

"'No, sir' what, Lester. Explain yourself." His voice is now much calmer. He is in the driver's seat.

"No, I'm not going against your orders. I was just thinking that company funds may be put to better use elsewhere. That was all, Mr. Pickersgill."

"Well, don't give it a second thought." He smiles like a stern but caring father. "I'll make sure the company pays for the therapist fees plus expenses. The last time I looked, the human resources budget for personnel development was flush with money. I'm sure I can get you a substantial bonus for extra time after regular office hours. Even if the company doesn't have the resources, I would pay for your sessions out of my own pocket. I have always had a lot of respect for your people. You're diligent, hard workers. That's why I prefer hiring Chinese."

9

Back at my apartment, when I awake, I'm surprised to find that I have dozed off for a while. The squat digital clock reads 6:14 PM. I must have slept for at least an hour.

I'm tired from the confrontation with Mr. Pickersgill in front of Clarissa Woo. There's something about those steely eyes of Clarissa and about her saucer face that angers me so easily. I think she may have even enjoyed seeing me, this Canadian born Chinese, squirm because I had to take the same speech training in English as she had to take.

Anyway, enough of that. There's still this coming Friday to deal with. I've got to find a woman to bring home some-how. Maybe I should take up my cousin Jeff's invitation to his church thing tonight. I think it's tonight, the college and careers fellowship at the Chinese First Non-denominational Evangelical Church of Toronto which the congregation affectionately refers to as the CFNEC. They call themselves the Timothy Fellowship named after the young pastor that St. Paul wrote to in the first century church.

I do remember meeting a nice Chinese Canadian girl

there named Lily Mah when I tagged along with my cousin Jeff and his wife Louisa on a few occasions.

I phone Jeff.

"Hey, Lester. Good to hear from you!"

"Jeff, I think I'll take you up on the church thing. I believe it's still on Wednesday evenings, isn't it?"

"Sure thing, Lester. It's on tonight. I'm glad you called. You won't regret it one bit. Plenty more women there now than when you last visited the fellowship. Actually we've split off into three different fellowship groups now."

"Oh yeah, sounds exciting. I assume it still starts at eight?"

"That's right. Do you remember, Lily Mah?"

"Sure I do. The one with the Rita Hayworth hair-do."

"Where have you been? All the women you're in love with are either in the movies or dead. You ought to get out more."

"Anyway, you're about to say something about Lily."

"Guess what, cuz?"

"I don't know. What?"

"She dumped Fred last Christmas. I think she has the hots for you."

"Shit, Jeff! Come on, give me a break." Secretly, I'm happy to hear that she's still interested in me, even though, I may be on her hit list of heathens for conversion to the faith.

"I'm just joshing you. You got to learn to loosen up a bit, Lester. Need a ride? Louisa and I can give you a lift tonight, if you like."

"No thanks. I'll drive up myself." I decide not to take public transit like I've been doing for a while. I'm thinking Lily may want a lift home after the fellowship meeting.

~~~
~~~

Before I head off to the evangelical fellowship, I go to my parents for supper. All the family's there tonight, my brother Dwayne, my sister Julie and her *lo fan* boyfriend Bruno.

Just when everyone is content with eating, Julie opens her mouth. "So are you bringing anyone to Pa's birthday this Friday, Dwayne?"

"Nope."

"What about that girl you've been seeing in New York?

"Julie!" A look of frustration and betrayal comes across my brother's face. "I told you not to bring it up in front of Ma."

"Come on, Dwayne. It'll be a nice change to actually see one of the girls you date."

"What girl," my mother says in Chinese. She looks lost whenever her children talk in English.

"Shit, Julie. You promised not to mention it in front of Ma."

"She doesn't understand what we're babbling about in English, Dwayne."

"She can guess. She's fairly good at guessing. And besides, it's not New York City but Buffalo."

"That's what I meant. Be a sport. Why do I have to bring home my dates and you guys have these mystery lovers across the border. It's not fair."

"She's no mystery to me."

"I bet she's not."

"Julie, it's none of your business."

"That's the problem with this family. Nobody communicates with each other."

"We are talking. You're the one who's not listening. I told you not to talk about her in front of Ma."

Julie starts humming and singing "Buffalo Gal, why don't you come home tonight, come home tonight...."

"That's it Julie! I'm outta here! You little bitch!" Dwayne grabs his bottle of beer and gets up. My mother pulls him back down into his chair.

"Eat, Dwayne. Be happy. No fighting tonight," my mother says. She turns to Bruno and Julie, "Eat. Eat, Bruno. Good eh?"

"Sure thing, Mrs. Chang. I love your Chinese broccoli." And then as he downs his beer, Julie playfully jabs him in the gut.

"What about you, Lester? Are you going to bring home a nice Chinese girl," Julie says.

"Like Dwayne says, it's really none of your business, Julie. And besides, she may not be Chinese."

"Whoa! My big brother Lester's going out with a *lo fan*. I find that hard to believe." She lights up a cigarette.

My mother gives her a dirty look.

"Well, Pa smokes at the dinner table." Julie looks at our father and then puts the cigarette out in an ash tray on the table behind her. She turns back to me. She says, "Well, Lester, are you bringing someone or not?"

"Not sure at the moment. Maybe."

"What about that Fung girl. What's her name? Wilma. That's it. What about Wilma?"

"Like I said. I'm not sure who I'll be bringing."

"Don't take any offense at what I'm going to say, Lester. But you're really better off with a Chinese girl. I can't see how any Canadian girl would have the hots for you. You're too shy with woman in general, white women in particular."

"Who the hell gives you the right to tell me what kind of woman I like."

"It's not who you like but whether they like you, Big Brother."

"I've had enough of this bullshit. I'm not taking any more of this bull from you, Julie."

"I'm just telling it like it is, Lester. That's all. You're just born with a personality that's more Chinese than Canadian."

Dwayne says, "Give Lester a break. So he's shy with women. What's the big deal, Julie?"

"I'm not shy!" I shout. "Just because I'm not screwing around with anyone right now doesn't make me shy." I hate being called "shy," even though that's exactly what I am, shy. But the idea that shyness is subsumed under the heading of the quiet Chinese riles me to no end.

Silence follows except for the sounds of the munching of food and the gulping of beverages. Trying to be the consoling sister that she can be, Julie tentatively starts up the conversation again.

"So how's work, Lester?" Julie asks.

"Alright," I say. "My boss is sending me on a course."

"What kind of course is that?"

"Something to do with upgrading communication skills."

"I would imagine the company's footing the bill?"

"Yeah. All expenses paid."

My father smiles, revealing a silver-capped tooth. He says, "You young people have it much better than us old-timers from China. You can all speak English so well." He grabs my shoulder and squeezes it proudly.

10

Louisa greets me at the door of the old house behind Jeff and Louisa's church in Chinatown. Normally, she is very cheerful, full of bubbles and warmth. Tonight she is even more so, her teeth gleam whiter than usual.

"I'm so glad you can make it," she says. "Look who's here, everybody," she announces over her shoulder. "It's Jeff's cousin, Lester!"

What's strange about everyone in the living room is that they all speak English perfectly, without a trace of chineseness, but at the same time they all look as Chinese as can be.

There must be about three dozen young men and women gathered in the room, sitting roughly in a circle, many on the floor, lotus style. They have a spic and span look about them, a lively glow in their faces.

I make the obligatory rounds with Jeff and Louisa. They introduce me to an elder of the church and to the youth pastor Winston Kam Yu.

We are next all called to gather around Pastor Winston and hear him give a "devotion" out of the big Bible he holds in an unzipped brown leather casing. He gives a pep talk on winning more Chinese Canadians for Jesus Christ, and that this church is capable of carrying out its mandate to evangelize the CBCs—Canadian Born Chinese—because many in the congregation at the 9:30 morning service are themselves Canadian born or raised in Canada. Everyone is made to feel special here at the Timothy Fellowship. Most Chinese churches cater to the recent immigrants from Hong Kong. And CBCs feel out of place in them because they don't speak Cantonese. Nor do they fit in with Caucasian churches in spite of the good intentions of the congregations. But here at the Chinese First Non-denominational Evangelical Church, God has given a vision to some of its members to have a ministry catering to the special needs of the CBCs.

For a moment, I feel like I'm no longer alone, that there are others who feel the same as I.

When we break for refreshments, many of them gather around to shake my hand and welcome me. There is a warm feeling about all the hoopla.

I make my way towards Lily as soon as I can. Sitting with her legs tucked side saddle, dressed in a black sweat shirt and blue jeans, she looks more lovely than ever. She still wears her hair Rita Hayworth style and speaks softly. She smiles at me while looking me straight in the eyes. I sit down beside her.

"You're looking well, Lily."

"Good to see you again, Lester. Welcome back to the fellowship."

"The fellowship group has grown quite a bit since the last time I was here."

"Winston has a lot to do with its growth. He's an ABC, you know."

"What's an ABC?"

"American Born Chinese. He comes from Boston as an

intern youth pastor. The congregation like him so much that they bring their friends to hear him speak. He doesn't act like he's giving a sermon or lecturing down at you. He's so unpretentious. We all love him. Because the CBCs can identify with him, he can reach out to them. How do you find him, Lester?"

"He's a bit of a joker."

"That's one of his good qualities as a youth pastor. He has a great sense of humour. You ought to drop by on a Sunday service and see how dynamic his sermons are. Not a dull moment with Winston in the pulpit. He's always an engaging speaker."

I look over to the small crowd gathered around Winston and see Jeff beside him, sharing jokes, I suppose. Jeff sees me looking in his direction and gives me the thumbs up.

"Actually, I've been thinking about Christianity recently," I lie and feel terrible doing so.

"Really?" Her eyes widen, her arms crossing over her chest in excitement. "I've been praying that you would come back."

"I figure I should have been more open-minded about this whole Christianity business in the first place."

"That's great news. Maybe you would like to join our Bible study on Thursdays. There are a couple of non-believers there as well."

"Sounds great."

"You'll have the opportunity to ask all the questions you want. As a matter of fact Winston will be there this week as a resource person. He's so knowledgeable about the Scriptures."

Lily stands there like a high school girl even though she is almost thirty. I think she's happy to see me again. She touches me a couple of times on the elbows to let me know how excited she is to see me tonight.

"Lily, I think maybe we can have coffee or lunch together tomorrow and you can clarify a few theological issues for me like you used to do?"

"That sounds like an excellent idea, Lester. How about lunch then next week?"

"Why not tomorrow?"

"I'm very busy this week."

"What about Friday evening?"

"Sorry, Lester, but I'm getting back together with my old boyfriend on Friday."

That old boyfriend would be Fred Hong, an urban planner at city hall. He's one of the lost sheep who, along with the likes of me, her church targets for conversion. I know the guy. I even like him. He's the only one among the sheep who speaks his own mind. "We're all here just looking for a girlfriend," he would quip often to the guys whenever he used to drop in on the Timothy Fellowship. That's why I like him, cynical to the core, but I'm surprised he ever got through the front door with Lily. She has always made it clear to me that Christians ought not to be unequally yoked, meaning she will only marry a born-again Christian. Fred is as staunch in his atheism as she is in evangelical Christianity. Everyone is surprised that they have ever gotten as far as boyfriend-girlfriend. The big question is why that heathen and not the other heathen, namely me.

"I guess we'll talk theology another time." I sigh.

"Give me a call next week and we can get together and have that chat." She pulls out of her purse a business card showing her title as the Out Reach Coordinator for the Timothy Fellowship.

She looks like a little girl all excited about a field trip, full of anticipation.

"Sure thing," I say.

"Make sure you don't lose it."

"Sure thing." I'm already thinking of ways of losing her business card as soon as I get home.

She smiles wider. She's always pleasant. She's pleasant at baptisms. She would be pleasant even at funerals. I imagine she can be pleasant when she sticks a butcher's knife into my heart.

After I return "good-byes" to everyone, I walk outside into the cool night air. A prickly sensation crawls all over my scalp and I sense that a headache is in the making. I sit quietly in the car.

I watch the remainder of the fellowship step out of the old house where we met. Some of them are paired off, boy-girl. They are handsome couples; the women are especially attractive. A few of them recognize me from earlier and cheerfully wave to me. I nod my head at them.

In front of my car is parked a blue Volvo. A tall couple stand beside it. I recognize them from the fellowship. The young man's stature is athletic, forearms large and muscular, the buttons on his chest strained tight. The young woman has one of those haircuts in bangs which remind me of David Bowie's girlfriend in the rock album *China Girl*. Before they get into the Volvo, he gives her a firm squeeze on her perfectly shaped bum.

11

AFTER LEAVING THE TIMOTHY FELLOWSHIP, I drive to the Red Rose Cafe in East Toronto. I'll make it just before closing time. French fries and gravy along with a tall glass of fountain coke will make everything alright.

As I approach the cafe, I notice the neon sign has been repaired. The phrase "Good Fool" which was in neon is now "Good Food" as it was originally meant to be.

Inside the cafe, I sit myself down into a booth. There is no sign of Ken or any of the regular waiters. A young Chinese woman in her late twenties is sitting at the cash counter, powdering her nose, a beige compact case in hand. A skinny Chinese man wearing a pink Polo shirt comes up to me and hands me a menu. The menu looks newly laminated and bigger than the ones I've seen before at the Red Rose Cafe. When I open the menu, I'm surprised to see that it's half in Chinese characters.

"You like real Cantonese food?" The young waiter asks me. "You Chinese?"

"My parents are from Toisan."

"I ask the cook to cook Cantonese style for you. Real Chinese food."

"No thanks. I've made up my mind already. I want a plate, make that, a large plate of fries and gravy, and a large fountain coke."

The waiter looks perplexed at my order. He takes his time writing down the order and stopping to look it up in the menu. When he can't find it, he asks me to point it out in the menu. I flip the pages quickly to look for it but can't find it either.

"You know what I mean. All I want is a large plate of French fries and have the cook put gravy on top of it. Okay?"

"Sure," he says and goes back to meticulously writing down the rest of the order.

"And don't forget the coke."

"Sure."

Shortly, he comes back from the kitchen. "Sorry, sir," he says. "No more fries. The cook shut down deep fryer already. The woks are still hot. How about a rice dish? They are very good."

"How about a plate of mushroom fried rice."

"Anything else?"

"That's all. And don't forget the coke."

He brings me a red can of generic brand coke.

"Don't you serve fountain coke anymore?" I ask.

"Oh, we throw away old fountain machine. We are getting new one next week. The new machine will automatically mix the carbonated water and syrup."

"I see. Where's Ken tonight?"

"Ken Wong? Oh, he's retiring to spend more time with his grandchildren."

"He's sold his business?"

"That's right. He sold it to me. I am the new owner. My

wife and her brother are also partners." He nods his head in the direction of the Chinese woman at the cash counter.

My dish of fried rice is presented on a small oval plate like the ones Ken used to use for sandwiches. The dish looks alright, less greasy than the fried rice I've had in the past here at the Red Rose Cafe. But I've lost my appetite all of a sudden.

As I flip through the jukebox menu for Bob Dylan, I notice the paper note taped over the coin slot. "Out of Order," it reads. I look around for a working wallbox but they all have similar pieces of white paper taped over the coin slot as well.

I sip my coke out of the can and twist the plastic straw around my fingers.

~~~

Soon I am back on the streets again, cruising around downtown, up and down Church Street. I park in the alley near the big church and walk in front of the church building, a dark, lifeless shadow.

As I meander about the night along the busy street, I keep a look out for a woman who I think might enjoy hurting men. I'm not sure how such a woman might look, but I hope that I will find one tonight.

The possibility that one of those women standing along the sidewalk may be an undercover cop unnerves me. I've heard recently about a campaign to arrest and shame the johns along this street. But I don't know where else to go.

I just keep walking north.

"Want a date?" A tall woman with large pretty eyes calls out to me. I ignore her. I don't want to look like I'm too desperate. I'll size up the street scene first. As I walk on, I
~~~

see a Mercedes do a U-turn in a gap in the traffic and pull up beside the tall woman. The lone man in the car speaks with her briefly and she gets in and the Mercedes quickly speeds up the street.

A truck drives by me slowly and its passenger, a young fellow in a cowboy hat, pokes his head out the window and shouts, "Horny Chink!"

By the time I walk past the intersection of Gloucester and Church streets, a jeep drives by with half a dozen men jammed into it. When they shout "faggot," I realize I have walked too far north and it's time to walk back south.

I retrace my path back towards the old church where several women have congregated like a gaggle of geese at the foot of the stone steps. They are dressed in a variety of fashionable dresses which reveal just enough skin to make my imagination take off. There is a petite blonde in a blouse tied in a knot just above her belly button. And next to a traffic sign, stands a tall dark woman with a pair of beautiful legs in hot pants. Another wears a conservative outfit like women might wear at an old fashioned Methodist church service except her blouse is unbuttoned all the way down to the belt buckle.

I walk up to the petite blonde standing at the corner furthest away from the others.

"How much?" I ask in a clear voice.

"Where's your car?" She looks at me, sizes me up and down.

"Near the church," I say. I point to the alley slightly beyond the church building which appears to be more shadow than brick and mortar.

"One hundred one hour."

"Seventy."

"Ninety's my bottom."

"Okay. Follow me this way, but stay at least thirty paces behind me."

"Hey, I thought you're parked just around the corner here?"

"I just want to be discreet. We'll walk around a couple of blocks. I don't want to look too obvious about what I'm doing."

"That'll cost you."

"How much more?"

"Another twenty."

"Twenty! Just for a walk around the neighbourhood?" I almost shout but I catch myself from being too angry. Have to be calm. "Alright, alright. Let's get going."

I walk slowly, trying not to cause too much attention. I look back casually, hands in pockets, and see her walking slowly thirty paces behind me. She's smoking a cigarette.

Across the street, I recognize one of the prostitutes I normally do business with, a dark haired woman in a smart pant-suit outfit. For a moment, I regret not asking her out tonight. She looks a lot like a taller version of Wilma. But I feel it just wouldn't work with someone I know, even someone who's given me blow jobs before. I need to be with a stranger tonight for what I have in mind.

The night air is getting chilly.

Once around the two blocks and soon we arrive at my car parked in the alley behind the church.

"I don't smoke," I tell her, noticing she still has a cigarette between her fingers.

"No problem." She obediently pinches off the burning end of the cigarette and stuffs the unused portion back into her pack of cigarettes.

"I see you were raised by frugal parents. Mine are like that too. They don't believe in waste."

"You don't say."

And then for a long while we say nothing to each other.

I drive us to the motel in Downsview, a fairly lengthy drive. The motel is located inconspicuously among blocks of low rise industrial buildings. She appears irritated and keeps looking at her watch.

"You should have told me the motel is so far away."

"You'll like it. It's a four star job."

She rolls her eyes and then forces a smile as though she recognizes that the customer is always right.

Inside the motel room, in the yellow light glowing through old plastic lamp shades, she sets out the ground rules. "I want the money up front."

"I know that." It's my turn to be irritable. I've been spoiled by my regular prostitutes who let me pay at the completion of their services. I say, "I hope you have change for a twenty."

"Sure thing. I always carry small denominations and silver."

I pull out my wallet and drape six twenty-dollar bills onto her milky white hands. She hands me a ten-dollar bill.

"Mind if I have one more smoke before we begin?"

"No, please do." I now imagine her wearing a black SS uniform, unbuttoned at the front, and holding a coiled bull whip.

"I won't charge the time I'm smoking."

She's quite attractive. Her white blouse, tied in a knot at the front, and her black tight pants, remind me of someone out of a 1950s movie, like Doris Day in the movie *The Pyjama Game.*

I sit down on the bed and tap my knees with my fingers, humming some nonsense. When I look up she's half undressed, a cigarette dangling from the corner of her mouth.

"Hey!" I say.

"Got a problem?"

"Why are you undressing so soon? What's the big hurry?"

"Isn't that what you're paying me to do, to undress?"

"Not so fast. Come on! Put your clothes back on!"

She shrugs her shoulders and starts buttoning up her blouse. After she finishes her smoke, she removes an emery board from her purse and files her nails. "Tell me when you're ready."

"Shit," I say to myself and I say to her, "I'm ready."

"Good boy." She quickly unbuttons her blouse again. I want to ask her to command me to unbutton it slowly but let it pass, because I just can't be bothered anymore. The sight of the beige colour of her bra and panties is depressing. I hate the colour. Flesh tones are so blasé.

I sit down on the bed and hum some nonsense again.

"Come on. Why aren't you undressing?" She asks me. By now she's totally naked. Her nipples are the same colour as the rest of her pale skin, only a tone darker. They look stretched thin. Her pubic hair is like a delta of dry sand.

I quickly undress and slip underneath the bed covers.

Cigarette still dangling from her mouth, she gets into bed next to me.

"You smoke a lot," I say.

"I guess I do."

A hint of talcum powder is in the air. Maybe she has powdered herself with baby powder.

"I think I'm ready now."

"Ready for some fucking, eh? Just give me another minute to finish my smoke."

"Sure, no problem. Just that it's getting late."

"You know, I used to work in New York one time."

"Really? Meet any celebrities?"

"A few."

"Any movie stars?"

"Robert Redford once hired me for a blow job."

"No kidding."

"Really. No shit. Honest to God and cross my heart. But I didn't know who he was when we first met. A friend of mine was asked to do this trick who was some big name celeb., but she wasn't told who he was at the time. Unfortunately for her, she got sick before she got a chance to meet him and asked me to fill in for her. 'I'm on holidays,' I said. She insisted and said the money should be good."

"How much did you make that night?"

"Who's telling the story? Just hold your horses. I'll get to that soon enough."

"Sorry, just curious."

"Turned out the client was none other than Robert Redford. God! Was I nervous!"

"You must have been scared."

"To say the least. I was petrified at the very thought of giving Robert Redford a blow job."

"Did you recognize him when you first met him?"

"No, oddly enough, I didn't at first, but I thought he looked awfully familiar. I asked him if he was in the entertainment business. He said that he made movies. I said that he would probably look good in front of a camera. Then he said he did work in front of a camera but preferred to be behind the camera. More creative, he said."

"So when did you know he was the Robert Redford?"

"When he started groaning and moaning the name of the Virgin Mary."

"What?"

"I read somewhere before in some newspaper like the

National Enquirer that he calls out to our Lady whenever he makes love."

"No kidding!"

"Yep. That's the God honest truth. I'm not pulling your leg. That's what the newspaper said. When he called out to Holy Mary, I realized I was giving Robert Redford a blow job. That was when I just froze. Holy shit, I thought. This is Robert Redford I'm sucking off."

"Then what happened?"

"He calmed me down. He said he understood my nervousness. Just relax, take your time, he said to me. Really, he was very patient with me. Gave me two thousand smackeroos for the night."

"Generous, wasn't he?"

"Sure was."

"After it was all over, I worked up the nerve to ask him for his autograph."

"No way. Both of you naked and you had the guts to ask for his John Doe?"

"Yeah, that's exactly how it happened."

"Well, did he give you his autograph? Do you have it with you?"

"Sure he did."

"Can you show it to me?"

"Sure." After butting out her cigarette, she gets out of bed and goes over to her purse at the far end of the room. She has a beautiful little bum. Back in bed, she holds a little coiled notebook in hand and opens it to a blank page with a diagonal line of scrawled script, quite illegible to me.

"The real McCoy, eh?"

"Yeah, that's his signature."

I take the little note book into my hands and run my fingers over its yellowing edges and then on the signature itself, feeling the gouged paper where the signature made its mark. The writer, whoever he or she might be, has a strong pen. I say, "His signature looks funny for some reason."

She ignores my remark. "Want to do some fucking now," she says.

"I'm ready as I ever will be."

"Stay calm," she says and gets up on her knees and straddles me. After she pulls away the bed cover she gives me a blow job.

When several minutes have passed, she says, "Feel anything yet?"

"No. I think...."

"Shshsh. Keep quiet. Let my fingers do the walking."

She gives me an old fashioned hand job. "Anything yet?"

"Nope."

Fatigue begins to show on her face. "Show me how you normally whack off," she asks me.

"Eh?"

"You know, show me how you masturbate."

"Oh," I say. I move my fingers like the crawling legs of a daddy-longlegs spider.

"God, I've never seen the likes of that," she says. "How do you do that?"

"It's easy. Make a circular motion like this. It's like you're picking an arpeggio on a guitar."

She's truly perplexed, biting her lower lip. "I don't think I can duplicate that. It must have taken a lot of practise," she says. "Let's try something else." She gets up out of bed again and goes to her purse to retrieve a can of ginger ale. After swallowing the first gulp, she holds the second gulp of ginger ale in her mouth and tries to give me a blow job with the mouthful of the evanescent pop. It tingles but I still can't get aroused. Then she tries again to jerk me off manually until she begins to get tired and continues a bit longer with one hand propped against her cheek and elbow on the bed.

"Let's take a break," she finally says.

"Okay by me."

She lights up a cigarette. And as an afterthought, she says, "You don't mind, do you?"

"No problem, go ahead."

With a hand under an elbow and the other holding a cigarette, she pauses to reflect. "What turns you on, eh ...? What is your name?"

"Lester."

"Well, Lester, what turns you on?"

"What's your name?"

"Just call me Cheryl. What gives you a hard on, Lester?"

"I want to be whipped right now."

"Besides that." She appears annoyed, mouth slightly curved inward. "There must be something else that turns you on."

"Nothing else right now. I feel all numb inside."

"How does your wife or girlfriend turn you on?"

"I don't have either one."

"Oh, you make love to virgins mostly?"

"No." I'm puzzled at that last remark but I let it pass. "I've never made love to anyone before, unless you count those occasions when I had to pay for sex."

"Why don't you imagine me as someone else, someone you love, someone you would want to do it with."

"I can't think of anyone right now. That's a tough one."

"Come on, Lester. There must have been some high school love or some college gal in your past."

"Honestly, I can't think of anyone at the moment."

"Lester, it's not uncommon for a guy to have problems from time to time. Just learn to relax. Here, I'll help you."

She gets me to sit up on the end of the bed and she kneels behind me. "Relax. Take it easy. Close your eyes." She then holds my head between her palms like between clamps of a vice, loosely at first and then gradually applies pressure. Her breasts are cold against my back. The smell of baby powder is still in the air. "Close your eyes now. Just relax. Let go."

The pressure on my head comes and goes in rhythm with her breathing, and slowly I become more relaxed. She massages my scalp from time to time.

"Lay down, now," she says. "But keep your eyes closed."

Gently, she massages my head, then the shoulders. It is a while before she sits on my belly and begins kissing me on the chest, working her way around one of my nipples. She bites it. I let out an "ouch!" She says, "Don't open your eyes. Imagine that I am the one woman you always wanted to make love with. Come on. You can do it."

"Honestly, Cheryl, I can't think of any woman that I would want to screw at this moment." It dawns on me that I've never wanted to make love with just one woman. I've always wanted to screw not just one woman but certain categories of women. I want to screw blondes who have slim builds. Or maybe brunettes with short hair. Or Chinese girls who speak perfect English. What I want to fuck is not a woman but the abstracted notion of a class of woman with specific features. Now I'm depressed.

"What's the matter Lester?"

"Eh? What do you mean?"

"You look pale all of a sudden like you've seen death."

"I don't know what has come over me but I can't get it up."

"Don't worry. Like I've said, a lot of men go through a phase like yours. Nothing to worry about. I think it's about time to call it quits for tonight, Lester."

"I'll pay you another twenty."

"Well…"

"Make it thirty for another fifteen minutes."

"If you put it that way. We'll give it another go."

I ask her to be rough on me. She bites my nipples again and slaps me a couple of times in the face. She even tries choking me with nylons. But nothing can arouse me tonight.

The fifteen minutes go by quickly. She turns her digital watch towards me. It is 2:30 AM already. I've forgotten to make a mental note of the time when we started counting the extra fifteen minutes.

"Sorry, Lester. It's time to go," she says.

She is fully clothed before I know it. Her hands on her hips, she stands astride. "Come on, hurry up."

"Coming."

After I'm dressed, she asks me, "Aren't you forgetting something?"

I look at my clothes and around the room. "I don't think so."

"The thirty dollars?"

"Oh yeah," I say, searching my back pocket for the wallet. "Here's twenty. Another five. Twenty-five. Just hold on a second." I dig deep into my shirt pocket and discover a two-dollar bill. "I'm sure I have some loonies somewhere on me." I look at her as she taps an elbow impatiently, cheeks sucked in, making her appear more sinister than I've noticed before. I find some loose change in my front trouser-pocket and count three dollars' worth.

"Thanks," she says.

Soon we are back in my car. I agree to drop her off at a transit stop on my way home.

"Here's my phone number," she says and hands me a piece of paper ripped out of the coil notebook. "Give me a call any time and we can do business again. Okay, Lester?"

"Sure." I take the paper with her phone number. I offer my hand to her. We shake hands. I've never really taken a close look at her face until right now. She must have wiped off some of the makeup before we left the motel room. Her facial skin is dry. Crows' feet radiate from the corners of her eyes. Then an impulse hits me. I lean over and kiss her on the mouth. I just have this urge to feel if she is real, if her lips are soft and sweet. And now I know. They are both.

She looks surprised. Eyebrows rise slightly. "What's that for," she says, eyes alert.

"I've never kissed a woman on the lips before."

"You don't say. I've never been kissed on the lips by a client before. Not with my clothes on, anyway."

12

THE NEXT DAY, THURSDAY, I wake up late. I phone in sick. It is almost noon and I feel like a burnt out cigarette. I need to get some fresh air, go for a walk. Something may yet happen to me, something good.

I put on my fedora and pretend I am Indiana Jones heading out for some adventure. Maybe along the way I will be captured by Amazon women and tortured, but not to death. That would be nice. It would make my day.

Hands in the pockets of my baggy shorts, I walk south. As I look up at the towering high-rises nearby, I wonder if there is a couple in one of those apartments right now making wild love, groaning and moaning when no one can hear.

In a neighbourhood known as The Annex, I come to this sidewalk cafe with a tacky, hand-painted sign of a roast chicken. This is not the first time. I come here occasionally for one reason: the barbecue chicken.

I seat myself at one of those little round tables for two near the large mural of the Garden of Eden scene in which a grey serpent wraps itself around Eve, covering her private parts, leaving a bit of dark nipple peering over the curve of the reptile. Here I sit during the sixth year before the end of the second millennium and at age thirty-four without a girlfriend, without the possibility for a lover in sight.

A waitress with a pale complexion and black short dress walks up to my table. She wears a nose ring. Her hair is a bleached blond that reminds me of near death encounters.

"What are you having?" She speaks in a monotone.

"Barbecue chicken," I say.

"Sorry. No have." She minces her mouth and stares at me and then finally looks away for relief. I'm not sure if that's the way she speaks normally or if it's for my benefit.

"Do you mean that you don't have any kind of chicken or that you only don't have barbecue chicken?"

"We don't serve chicken."

"I have been here many times," I exaggerate. "And besides, doesn't that sign say chicken."

"No, it doesn't say anything. It is only a painting of a chicken."

"But it signifies chicken surely."

"Symbols have no meaning." She quickens. She's on familiar ground.

"But this restaurant has always served barbecue chicken for as long as I can remember."

"Well, we don't anymore. It's strictly vegetarian now. Is there anything else you want to order?" She examines the finger nail on her little pinkie and then looks at me.

"What would Kafka think about all this bullshit?" I stand up to leave and I realize how pretentious my remark is. I've never read Kafka but have a notion that it may be appropriate to toss at a woman dressed in black, wearing a nose ring and who refuses to serve me barbecue chicken.

My eyes follow the curve of her body as she walks away to serve a couple at the next table. A tuft of auburn hair springs forth like a star burst from beneath her white arm-pits as she lifts her arm to point at the chalkboard menu on the brick wall. She smiles at the man with the dark pony tail sitting with, I guess, his girlfriend, a pixy blonde in a paisley dress. Then the waitress laughs at something he has said. She ignores his date as she places her hand on his shoulder. Meanwhile, his date in the paisley dress continues looking at the menu.

With hands in pockets, I meander towards Koreatown on this hot summer day. As I weave my way through the crowd, I keep my eyes open for mixed couples, particularly the Chinese-Caucasian combination. I want to confirm my theory that there are more Chinese women hitching up with white guys than the other way around. By the time I reach the Christie subway station, I count eleven couples that I suspect are Chinese-Caucasian, and among eight of them, the female is Chinese.

I'm not sure why, but a sudden pang for authentic Chinese food hits me. My mouth waters for a bowl of wonton and noodles at one of those dives in the Spadina and Dundas area usually run by Hong Kong immigrants. Normally, I avoid them. But at the moment, I am at a loss where else to eat.

In those restaurants, the customers, who are alone or in small groups, are expected to share a big round table with other customers when it is busy. Like the repertory movie houses, those greasy dives in Chinatown seem to attract not too infrequently lone white women who would casually sit at one of those big tables with strangers, often with Chinese people who seem to speak only Chinese. I don't know why this is so about the attraction of foreign films and authentic Chinese food. Maybe it's merely a yearning for something exotic, a safe escape from boredom.

Queen's Noodles on Spadina I've been to before, so I decide to eat there. Cool air blasts me in the face as soon as I enter the restaurant. The scent of oyster sauce and sesame seed oil fills the air.

Even though it is now long past the noon hour rush, the place is almost a full house. A few of the white customers remind me of the hippies from the sixties or early seventies in their tie-die shirts and sandals. They order dishes like the Chinese would order: squid, steamed lettuce with oyster sauce, and beef tripe as well as the more familiar wonton and noodles in a steaming broth. A Caucasian couple shares a big table with several Chinese men.

Many of the Chinese patrons bow their heads close to their bowls and plates as they eat their meals as though in prayer. The sound of slurping confirms that they are not in fact praying but eating.

A Chinese girl with a blackish-blue mole on her cheek comes around the cash register after giving a customer his change and says to me, "One," in English. I'm the only Chinese guy whom she speaks English to that I know of. The only time she spoke Cantonese to me was when I first came into this restaurant a couple of years ago. After listening to my Toisan dialect, she has spoken English to me ever since.

I point to the corner table and sit down with my back to the red altar resting on a high shelf at the back of the room next to the kitchen. Joss sticks protrude out of a little pot on the altar. Three figurines of men in long flowing robes and long black whiskers stand guard beside the altar.

The waitress with the mole plops a red menu in front of me and another brings me a tin pot of Chinese tea. The latter takes my order for a large bowl of wonton and noodle soup. She carefully records the order on her yellow newsprint pad and walks briskly to the front where the cooks are steaming dumplings and noodles next to the entrance.

I wipe my tea cup, porcelain spoon, rice bowl and chopsticks with a paper napkin just as my mother had taught us to do whenever we ate out in Chinese restaurants.

An old balding Chinese man at the table next to mine folds his red menu and looks up. A waitress takes his order. In familiar Toisan dialect, the old man orders a bowl of rice with barbecue duck. The waitress contorts her face and repeats the order in Cantonese along with commentary, drawing out each vowel, stressing each diphthong and raising her eyes and nose above his bald head. The old fellow bobs his head up and down in agreement and licks his lips. He does not smile but neither is he upset about anything. He appears contemplative as he looks across the room and blinks a couple of times.

Through the front door enters a party of six women. They are directed to sit at the very front table. They look familiar and I can't remember where I have seen them until the seventh one comes in to join them. It is Tiffany once again, I think to myself. No, on second thought, she's not Tiffany, but she looks a lot like her. Her golden halo of hair is restrained into a pony tail. It has the same crinkly texture about it as that of Tiffany's. But her bum is heart shaped like Wilma's. Yes, only a bigger version of it. Her face, it is identical to Lena Olin's. The legs are definitely Kathleen Turner's, circa the premiere of her role in *Body Heat*.

At first, I turn my face away, taking quick peeks at her from time to time, sipping from my glass of tea, using the glass tumbler to obscure my face.

On a folded napkin, I start to compose a poem, "I cannot live without you...." and tear it up immediately. She deserves more. I must pay her for making me feel like a Chink. For making me visit prostitutes. If only she would return my love I would be rid of my desire for self-flagellation.

I can visualize her blue eyes glittering as I penetrate her in some dark alley. This one for the Queen Mother, this one for multicultural policies that welcome ethnics indiscriminately, this one for...this one for not understanding my perfect English spoken in a slur because my chinkiness precedes my voice.

First, I must get a photograph of her to meditate on.

I wait until they are finished eating, the Lena Olin lookalike and her friends. I follow them, keeping my distance until they go their separate ways at the St. Patrick Station. She takes the north bound train with one of her female friends. I enter the same subway car behind a crowd. A little old lady stands next to me, her face almost at my armpit level. She looks up at me and I can smell garlic from her breath. It seems everyone is sweating in the train.

The woman with the Lena Olin face grasps one of the steel poles in the middle of the train. I can see her white armpits, freshly shaven. They are smooth and white.

She leaves her friend and transfers to the east bound Danforth train at St. George. I'm glad for the huge crowd today. Like a winding serpent the crowd flows from one train up over stairs and down over another set and into the east bound train. At Donlands, she gets off and walks several blocks to a low rise building.

I follow her twenty, thirty paces behind. There are still many pedestrians on her way home. Thank God for rush hours. When I see her standing at the front door and looking in her purse, I slow down my walk. By the time I am standing almost right behind her, she finally gets the door open.

I pretend that I'm looking at the name list. She looks

at me and smiles. I smile back and contemplate asking a question but I don't know what to ask.

"Looking for a friend?" She says.

"Yeah."

"What's his name?" She adds, "Or her name?"

"Eh, well...Bob."

"I don't recollect anyone living here by that name or even Robert." She squints and pats her Kathleen Turner thighs. "What's his last name?"

"I don't remember. Eh...We met just yesterday."

"Oh, I see. I'm sorry. I can't help you there. Gotta go."

"Oh?"

"I hope you find your friend."

She leaves me standing outside but lucky for me I have the alertness of mind to jam the door open with my foot. I watch her happily walk through the lobby and make a right turn. While I pause for her to disappear around the far corner before I follow her, she then suddenly comes back to me. She asks, "Your friend, he didn't say which floor he might be living on, did he by chance?"

"No. No, he didn't mention anything about the floor he lives on."

"I just thought of someone on the first floor who kind of looks like a Bob type. Just a thought. Good luck."

"Thanks."

By this time a huge biker type, with a beer gut, saunters out of the doorway passing by the woman with the Kathleen Turner thighs. He slows to a standstill at the door. I act like a doorman at the Royal York Hotel and wave him through. He keeps his eyes on me as he steps outside.

"I'm just looking for a friend," I say to him.

The biker doesn't say anything and just continues to look at me as I slip into the lobby of the apartment. When he finally turns around, after what seems like the time it would have taken to find Santa Claus, I dash on tip toes in the direction where the woman with the heart-shaped bum has disappeared. All I can see is an empty hallway with about twenty apartment units and a staircase to my right. The dust and mildew in the air remind me of the hallway in the motel last night as though the place hasn't been vacuumed for some time. I go up the stairs, two steps at a time, and find myself in a hallway identical to the first one, empty as well, except for an elderly couple coming out of the end unit.

I take the subway back to my own apartment to pick up my camera. I then drive up to the nearby drugstore and buy three rolls of film. At a Canadian Tire store, I buy fifteen feet of nylon rope. In the parking lot, on the way back to the car, I remember once watching an episode of "Raw Hide" where a cowboy threatens to whip an Apache with a piece of rope soaked in a bucket of water. They didn't have nylon in the Wild West, I reckon. So I go back to the store after I drop the coil of nylon rope into the trunk and toss the film in the glove compartment of my car.

When I go back to the hardware section, I discover the spindle for the cotton rope is empty. I ask a clerk for ten feet of cotton rope.

"Sorry, sir, but we sold our last length of cotton rope a week ago," the sales clerk in the hardware department says to me. The fullness of the red in her hair is in stark contrast to the wrinkles on her face. I suspect that she may be wearing a red wig to hide the fact she might be a grandmother.

"What? Where am I going to get ten feet of cotton rope at this hour? I thought you guys always keep everything in stock," I say.

"Well, we normally do but for some reason cotton rope

sold like hot cakes this month. But if you like you may call us next week. Another shipment of rope should be in by then."

"I was counting on ten feet of cotton rope now."

"May I interest you in perhaps one of our other brands? We have cords made of hemp or rattan as well as nylon."

In her ponderous but methodical steps, the lady clerk walks to the spindles of cords and ropes. Her breasts seem monstrous on her stocky little frame.

"How about this hemp cord? Will that do for your purpose?"

I take it and lash it across the back of one hand.

"It doesn't hurt one bit. No, it won't do."

"What do you mean by that?"

"Oh, it's kind of embarrassing. I mean. Gee."

"Don't say another word. I'll never understand what you young people do for kicks these days. Sharing a double-frosted-malt together is just not enough excitement for kids these days."

"What the heck. I'll take ten feet of the hemp cord."

I am just relieved to get out of that store with my rope.

Parking my car in front of the apartment where I last saw the woman with the Lena Olin face, I prepare to wait all night for her to come back out. For a moment I panic, thinking I may have bought the wrong film. But luckily, when I look at the boxes, "400 ASA" is printed on two of them and "100 ASA" on the other, just as I had wanted.

By about midnight, my stomach is growling again. The battle between the lusts is on, between hunger and libido. I fantasize how she would look, stripped to the waist, dripping in sweat. Thick ropes bind her hands. She dangles in the darkness of her own apartment while I inflict the pain of wet cords whipping across her tender back. I imagine how she might feel, helpless and yet wanting pain. Love and torture will kiss each other, intermingle like blood and sweat.

At the same time, in my mind, the smell of roast pork leads to an uprising of the senses. I can taste the sweetness of marbled meat, thin layers of fat interleaving layers of meat, topped with crisp, fragrant pork rind. The warmth rises to my face from an imagined plate of steamed rice.

As I look at the empty street lit by the violet light of mercury street lamps, I feel the futility of tonight. I allowed my "Lena Olin" to slip by me.

But when a white police cruiser slowly rolls past me, two moustached cops looking at me, my decision is sealed. I drive back to the Queen's Noodle House on Spadina and satisfy my hunger. The fulfilment of my sexual fantasy will have to be deferred once again.

As soon as the waitress brings me the large plate of roast pork and steamed rice I begin stuffing myself so quickly I can barely breathe. The pork is not salty enough so I pour plenty of soya sauce onto the pieces of pork. I stir the rice to soak up the sauce and what little natural juices there are. I find my chest heaving with exhaustion. But still feeling unsatisfied and empty, I ask for the menu again. I haven't had wonton and beef brisket soup for a while so I put in an order for a large bowl. I devour the big chunks of beef, including tendons and every bit of fat. People stare at me as I suck up the wontons into my mouth, making slurping noises as the noodle wrap on the wontons is siphoned into my mouth. When I finish eating, I'm exhausted, panting as I sit with my head thrown back.

13

AS I DRIVE ONTO THE bridge over the Don Valley Parkway, I almost fall asleep at the wheel. A bump on the pavement keeps me awake.

There is a lonely figure standing on the middle of the walk way on the bridge. The tacky dress which the woman is wearing evokes something familiar. As soon as I cross over the bridge, I feel compelled to turn onto a side street. After I park my car, I walk onto the bridge.

The wind blows cold tonight, not the cold of autumn yet but a chill nonetheless, perhaps an omen of the kind of autumn to come.

As I walk closer to the silhouette of the lone woman, I soon realize she's wearing a plastic green overcoat, like one of those discards that can be bought at any discount store.

We stand about three giant steps from each other, she staring into the dark and at the southbound traffic beneath, and I, looking at her profile.

"Maureen?"

"Hello Lester," she says without looking at me. She clasps

tight a small white purse. I can see the sinews in her hands, even in this dim light.

"Yep, that's me," I say, feeling stupid, not knowing what else to say. "I didn't know if it's you or not, but I sort of recognized your dress, I mean your coat."

"I've never worn this coat to the office before. How could you have seen it before tonight?"

"It has the same style as your other clothing." I catch myself suddenly in another gaffe.

"My wardrobe is rather cheap looking, isn't it?"

I scratch my head, not sure if she's being sarcastic or what. "It's the person who's wearing the clothes, that matters, not the clothes," I say.

She looks at me when I say this and then she sucks in her lower lip briefly, and turns her gaze back onto the oncoming traffic.

"A bit chilly for a walk tonight isn't it," I say.

"I suppose you're right at that."

The wind blows her hair back like ribbons waving in the air. The hair looks greasy and grimy. I recognize a strange odour, like salted fish, about her when I walk up to her downwind. She turns as she follows my movement until her back is toward the oncoming traffic. She leans back against the guard rail. I raise a hand to grab her but stop when she holds herself upright and steady against the rail. I'm grateful for my slow reflexes.

Her face is eerie in the street light. Drops of perspiration mark her forehead.

"I think you're going to catch a cold if you stay out in this weather any longer, Maureen."

"And die of pneumonia? That's not a bad idea at all, Lester. Thanks."

"My car is just around the first corner past the bridge. I'll give you a ride home."

"Say my name again."

"Maureen?"

"Say it again."

"Maureen."

"That's better."

"Can we go now? It's getting late. You've got work tomorrow."

"No, I don't."

"Come on, Maureen. Stop kidding around."

"Would I kid you, Lester?"

"Let's go. You'll feel better in the morning."

"It is morning now."

"I mean when you wake up."

"Nobody wakes up in this nightmare."

I ignore her remark although it catches me by surprise. Maybe we are all living in our own heads, nobody seeing things as they are but as they wish to see them. Sounds like hell to me.

Gently pulling her at the elbow, I encourage her along the walk over the bridge to my car. Halfway there, she clutches my arm and leans against me.

Inside the car, the sweat clings to her blouse and to her hair. "We're going home, now," I say.

Soon the car is winding its way down to the Bayview Extension underneath the very bridge she was standing on when I first saw her a little while ago. The dark outline of the bridge looms overhead as we make our way back to her place.

Inside her townhouse, I can smell a trace of fillet of sole. The living room is a mess. Two shelves of a book case are emptied, their books haphazardly piled on the floor beneath it. A photograph of a handsome, rugged man looks at me through a cobweb of splintered glass.

"I guess World War III came early for you," I say.

"Sorry about the mess."

"No problem. I'm just talking off the top of my head. Let's get you to bed."

"I can't sleep."

Her eyes are red and watery. Her face is flushed pale. I believe her. She is too wired up.

"I'll make you some hot milk. That'll get you to sleep."

In the kitchen, dirty dishes cover the sink. There is not even a clean cup in the cupboard. The same goes for the pots. So I wash a lipstick stained mug from the sink.

After making her a cup of hot milk, I say, "I think you may have to call in sick tomorrow. You don't look all that well."

"Sure." She holds the mug with both hands. A bit of colour is coming back to her face now.

As though prompted by an afterthought, she takes out a plastic pill bottle from her purse. The bottle is orange tinted with no label. She takes two capsules and pops them into her mouth and swallows with the milk.

Not knowing what else to say, I tell her, "I'll be going. I'm beat."

"Be a dear and get me a smoke, will you, Lester?"

"Where do you keep your cigarettes?"

"Over there in the cassette tape box on the stereo shelf." I notice for the first time the arm on the old fashioned turn-table is torn off, blue, red, white wires reaching out like veins and arteries.

With a smile, the first one tonight, she accepts the ciga-rette from the opened Players Light box I offer her.

The next five minutes or so, we search the room for

matches. She doesn't have a lighter. She prefers the feel of matches between her fingers and the smell of sulphur, she says. Failing to find any matches, I suggest to her we can try lighting the cigarette on one of the electrical elements on the stove. She moves toward the kitchen but I stop her and take the cigarette from her. "I'll do it. You might singe your hair." The stove element is hotter than I thought but I manage to light one cigarette and nearly choke on the smoke.

"Here," I say. My eyes are watering.

"Thanks." She takes a long draught on it. Curling up her legs on the long sofa, she says, "Thanks again for being there."

"Where?"

"On the bridge tonight. And for all the times you've been so kind to me, putting up with my whining, listening to me and not judging me."

"No big deal."

"Why do I always get hitched with the assholes of the world?" She says as she massages her forehead with her palm. Then she looks up at me. "I got a letter from Matt."

"Yeah?"

"He sent a photograph along with it. You can never guess what's on it."

"What's on it?"

"It's a picture of him and his new girlfriend sun bathing in the Bahamas."

"Oh?"

"The bastard and his bitch. Would you treat your girl-friend that way? Even if she's an ex?"

I shrug my shoulders and just sit there on the sofa next to her, wanting to say that she may rest her head on me, but I'm too shy to speak up.

"Am I that ugly? Is there a sign on my forehead saying Use and Discard?" She says. Her lower lip starts quivering and then her entire face grimaces and breaks into crying. For a moment her crying appears more like a distorted sort of laughter. Instinctively, I hold her hand.

Then she hugs me and I let her. Tears wet my shirt, a few tear drops stream down my chest and I shiver with a strange chill.

She lifts up her head and looks at me with brown eyes, eyes I've never taken notice of before, eyes warm and welcoming. She has dimples too. It's as if I am only now seeing her face for the first time.

I want to make love with her but I'm frightened.

She unbuttons the top button on the front of her dress. I grab her wrists. My fears have won out, my fear of women, my fear of white women. "Please, don't," I say. I get up and rush into the bathroom.

Inside, I lock the door, pushing it a couple of times to make sure it's properly closed. I strip to the waist in front of the mirror. With one of the lipsticks from the medicine cabinet I scrawl in capital letters the word *CHINK* across my chest.

I whisper to the man in the mirror, "Chink. You Chink. Why would she want you?"

Maureen calls out from the living room. "Lester, are you alright in there?"

"I'm okay," I say in a voice so calm that I find it hard to believe it as my own. "It's something I ate earlier today." She sounds like she accepts my excuse to lock myself in the bathroom.

Then I roll onto my side and curl up on the floor as I cry. My throat strains as though I'm screaming but no sound can come out of my mouth. But I hear the words within my head: "Useless Chink. Useless Chink. Useless Chink." After I stop crying, I stretch out onto my back and stare at the ceiling. On the ceiling a yellow-brown water stain in the shape of an angel hovers over me. At that moment I acknowledge who I am. I am a Chink, pure and simple. And someday, I may become a Chinaman like my father, my dear father. That's not too bad, is it? Settle down. Raise a family. What's wrong with that? And in the process learn to love your wife.

I wipe the red lipstick off my chest with soap and wet toilet paper. After putting on my shirt and flushing the toilet paper in the toilet, I go back out to the living room. Maureen has fallen asleep, dry lips, mouth opened, on the long sofa. Her hand on the arm rest holds a smouldering cigarette, ashes on the verge of falling. I gently take the cigarette by the filter tip and accidentally drop half the ashes onto the carpet before I put it out in the ash tray. I get on my knees and carefully shovel clumps of the ashes with a brochure I find lying on the coffee table.

After looking around to make sure there are no sparks from her cigarette, I go into her bedroom and retrieve a blanket off her unmade bed. I lay the blanket over her, covering her from neck to toe. On a note pad I find in the kitchen, I write in large letters my home phone number and my office extension, and a message that she may call me for anything. I underline *anything*. I leave the note on the coffee table next to her.

As I open the front door to leave, I realize there's no way of locking the door after I step outside, so I close it again and lock it. I don't remember where she put the keys. I'll stay the night and curl up on the armchair across from where Maureen is sleeping.

When dawn has broken and I'm awake, I make instant coffee for myself, holding the hot cup in both hands as I sit in the kitchen alone.

After I wash my coffee cup, I gently shake her shoulders to wake her and tell her that I have to leave to go to work. Between tired eyelids, she peers at me. I apologize for waking her but ask her to lock the door behind me. But before I leave, I tell her where I left a note with phone numbers where I can be reached. She says thanks, still in a half stupor.

I drive back home, shower and head off for work. The first person I meet in the office is Clarissa Woo. We exchange hellos. Then I say to her that Wednesdays are alright by me for our speech therapy sessions. Her thin eyebrows rise and then she tells me that Mrs. Fay, the speech therapist, had phoned yesterday and asked Mr. Pickersgill to let us see her for a preliminary session later this afternoon.

Clarissa and I have lunch together before seeing Mrs. Fay. My treat, I insist. We eat dim sum at this Cantonese restaurant. I hardly say anything while she tells me her family problems: mother-in-law not getting along with her, nanny returning to the Philippines, husband being demoted and eldest daughter hating her new school. While listening to Clarissa's woes, I lose my appetite.

After the preliminary tests at the speech therapy office, Mrs. Fay requests that she speak to each of us alone. In her assessment of me, she has diagnosed a speech impediment which will likely require a few more sessions than in the estimate she had given to Mr. Pickersgill. She will speak to Mr. Pickersgill about the extra sessions.

Back at the office I see the red light blinking on my phone to indicate a message. The recorded message is from Maureen. I phone her.

"How's it going?" I say.

"I'm feeling a lot better after I got my baby-sleep. I just want to tell you, I appreciate all that you did for me last night."

"I'm glad you're feeling better."

There is a pause. Then she says, "I'm embarrassed to say this." She pauses again. "I apologize for my behaviour last night, if I seemed a little strange. Actually, everything about last night is somewhat hazy right now. It's the drinking along with the pills I've been taking for my nerves. I can't seem to remember too clearly."

"That's alright."

There is another pause. There's something rustling at the other end, then a crackling noise, maybe static. "Did I ask you to go to bed with me last night?"

"Not in so many words, but you were behaving...how shall I put it...a bit forward."

"God—I'm really sorry if I acted like a lush."

"Don't worry. It's probably the pills. Forget it."

"Lester, thanks for not taking advantage of me. I really appreciate you for respecting me."

Before I hang up, I ask her if she's up to going to my father's birthday party. She politely declines, saying that she's not up to it. I promise to phone her later during the weekend and hang up the phone.

I open the bottom drawer of my desk and take out a can of spaghetti and meatballs. In the staff room, I stand in line behind three other office workers to use the microwave. As I wait patiently, I ponder the exquisite meal I am about to eat.

THE END

Doré Bak is the son of a couple from Hoiping, China. His grandfather first arrived in Canada from China during World War I and later got into bootlegging booze in Saskatchewan before settling in Alberta as a restaurateur. Doré is currently contemplating the exhaustion of the Protestant Reformation in the early twenty-first century. *Love Stalks* is his first published work of fiction.

www.ingramcontent.com/pod-product-compliance
Lightning Source LLC
Chambersburg PA
CBHW071008120726
47910CB00004B/1432